BIG
BLUE
LAVENDER GIRL

JUDY MAY

THE O'BRIEN PRESS
DUBLIN

First published 2006 by The O'Brien Press Ltd,
12 Terenure Road East, Rathgar, Dublin 6, Ireland.
Tel: +353 1 4923333; Fax: +353 1 4922777
E-mail: books@obrien.ie
Website: www.obrien.ie

ISBN-10: 0-86278-991-5
ISBN-13: 978-0-86278-991-6

British Library Cataloguing-in-Publication Data
May, Judy
Blue lavender girl
1. Teenage girls - Fiction 2. Young adult fiction
I. Title
823.9'2 [J]

1 2 3 4 5 6 7 8 9 10
06 07 08 09 10 11 12

The O'Brien Press
receives assistance from

Printed and bound in the UK by CPI Group

To Susie Hemsworth, so full of love

1, 2, 3, 4, 5, 6, 7, 8, 9, 10, 11, 12,
13, 14, 15,16, 17, 18, 19, 20, 21,
22, 23, 24, 25, 26, 27, 28, 29, 30,
31, 32, 33, 34, 35, 36, 37, 38, 39,
40, 41, 42, 43, 44, 45, 46, 47, 48,
49, 50, 51, 52, 53, 55, 56, 57, 58,
59, 60, 61, 62, 63, 64, 65, 66, 67,
68, 69, 70, 71, 72, 73, 74, 75, 76,
77, 78, 79, 80, 81, 82, 83, 84, 85,
86, 87, 88, 89, 90, 91, 92, 93, 94,
95, 96, 97, 98, 99, 100, 101, 102,
103, 104, 105, 106, 107, 108, 109

DAY 1

<#>

Oh forget it! Kira has this crazy idea that if you count to five hundred while imagining him kissing you, then the next time it has to happen. *Has* to. The energy you give it, or whatever, makes it so that the universe *must* deliver, and if you write it down then it's even stronger.

Kira is a bit 'out there' thanks to having swum with the dolphins on her holidays and now she fancies herself as a spiritual something-or-other.

It might work, the five hundred thing. My second cousin Susie tried it and ended up getting this guy called George. Problem is, each time I do it I keep changing my mind and imagining different guys. So by the time the party happens I'll be either alone, or what Mum would call a 'young hussy'.

I'll take hussy. No, actually, I haven't the energy, and it's not how I'd want them to finally notice me.

Kira and Dee's mums both went to a self-help seminar last week (my mum would never go to anything new like that) and bought us all these journals 'For Successful Living', and I've now been writing in mine for a full five minutes and don't feel any different. I don't give a crap about successful living, I'm just bored rigid because of this stupid power cut.

FACT: It takes fifteen candles to make enough light to just about read and write by.

FACT: Twelve of the candles have religious pictures on them and the others are actually mine. My mother is *so* embarrassing. She should have just been a nun and had done with it and then my dad could have married someone who would have forced him to be cool, instead of forcing him to go to church every morning. At least they've given up on making me go. My mum and dad are older than just about everyone else's by about, oh, a hundred years. I guess that's why they don't mind power cuts, it's nice and old-fashioned for them. I have just fought Dad off from putting geranium oil in these candles. Geranium oil smells of cat, and not in a good way.

I have been trying all day to work out how to be sick tomorrow. Problem is how to be sick for the exams and not so sick that I won't be able to stay over at Kira's on Friday.

Wait! Hold on! Just remembered, there's *no way* they'll let me go to Kira's after last week.

BACKGROUND: Kira's mum never got the parent note, or whatever, about how when teenage girls come to visit they are supposed to stay in the house, giggling in their daughter's bedroom. She also never got the other note about how, 'going down the road to the corner shop', secretly means, 'going into town to hang out for half the night'.

But then, mine believed me about Kira's house not having a phone, so for a while we just thought we could do what we wanted, that we were all being dragged up by idiots.

Then last Saturday night Mum and Dad came out of their big annual 'all the churches' meeting, and were walking to the parking garage just as me and the girls and some friends of Dee's brothers were walking back towards the cinema. Only ten miles from where I said I'd be and with a dozen more people.

Disaster, total, on so many levels, lots of shouting. Maybe they organised the power cut just to punish me. They were going to think of a big punishment, but then they forgot. I always felt OK about the stuff we did because I figured that I was getting punished already by having freaks for parents. Now the freaks have had a meeting with a counsellor and decided to take an 'active interest' in me, which means they ask me how I am all the time and recommend films that they can't quite remember the title of, but are apparently very good.

God, this *has* to end.

DAY 2

We have been finding bits of Aidan all over the house. Well, not actual bits of him, arms and ears and eyeballs, but stuff he probably meant to take with him.

I'm *sure* his pasta-maker was meant to make the trip with him, there's no way Mum would make a meal from anything other than a frozen thing. I imagine he will be king of his university because he can cook like on the TV shows where the chefs pile things up and drizzle stuff over it just in time, except he favours normal food over pheasant. It's a shame he's doing the summer classes first, otherwise he'd have been here for the holidays. I will now have to eat peanut butter and crackers for the next four years unless something drastic happens.

God, why am I even writing in this again? I mean, the lights are on today. They discovered a branch had fallen on the wires in front of next door's house and someone intelligently sent fifteen men in hard hats around to stare at it until a truck arrived.

It's a risky thing to do, to write down all the secret bits of you on paper. I've decided to write it on the wrong pages so if they find it then I can say, 'How can it be true? Look, that was the date I went to the dentist and not a mention of that!' Have to make sure free expression doesn't turn into damning evidence.

I only stayed for the first half of my last exam today. Anyway, I hate being around after exams, it just ends up with everyone comforting the class genius who thinks she missed one of the hundred questions on the test, and everyone else saying, 'I'm sure I failed', when they know they didn't.

I'm going to sort my clothes out tonight, maybe even wash some of them. At least I'll have weeks and weeks of being able to wear what I want and not be told that it is against approved school regulations. Who, tell me, was the smart ass who decided that wearing black all the time meant you were depressed? Imagine I made up a rule that wearing lilac meant you were a big fat liar. The lady two doors down would have to go naked as I'm sure her underwear is as lilac and matchy as her hats and coats. Her name is Mrs Traynor and she stops me every now and then to tell me to stand up straight and smile.

Now that I think of it, if we are freely giving orders to each other, what's to stop me telling her to pull the hat down over her face and shut up like a good little woman?

DAY 3

Last day of school. Huge relief. Massive.

This year they appointed a school psychologist so I've had to learn to look happy and well adjusted, at least while walking the halls. I know she has a file on me. Everyone who's been less than angelic in the past has a file on them somewhere.

It used to be that me, Kira and Dee would all end up in various offices together, because we were all out to do what felt right, not what they told us. But the two of them have gone a bit boring, like they want to fit in and suck up. I've got wise and I stay out of everyone's way, but at least I haven't given in and started doing what they want. For example, homework was invented so they could control us after school as well as during. Most of the teachers have given up asking me for it. I think they are secretly glad that I just avoid working and that I'm not one of the ones who acts up in class and says cheeky stuff.

I'm so proud of the fact that I have said *nothing* in any class for at least a month now.

I mean, look at them! What do they know? If I did what they told me to I would end up like them with their little jobs and little cars or like my parents with their meetings and services. No-one I know is really alive. I would love to know one person who does something amazing in the world.

It's me too, I'm as dead as the rest of them.

I don't say these things out loud anymore, so it's nice to write them here. A couple of months ago they sent me to a special Saturday morning Artistic Communication class, which lasted four weeks until some department ran out of money. They called it 'Artistic Communication', but we saw the 'art therapy' labels on all the boxes of paint supplies. I remember the first class. We had to draw how we feel on one side of the paper, and what we love to do on the other. I felt sort of nothing. I don't do that much either.

I remember two or three years ago I would do fun stuff and be really into it; one time I made a light-box out of my old dolls' house, and I used to love tracing pictures of birds and pop-stars onto typing paper. I also remember being big into a band that is *way* too embarrassing to write down here, in fact I think the pen would die of shame and I'd have nothing left to write with. I belonged to the fan club and everything, and Aidan would give me money for my birthday so I could get the calendar and photos – which I would carefully hide under my bed, as if anyone on earth would want to steal them! Actually, I've just looked and they are still there. Must clean my room. Really. Any year now.

I wish I was back the way I was then. I was really happy then.

There's one OK-ish-I-suppose thing – I'm *thrilled* they aren't sending me to an activity camp this summer. I feel that I will be no more employable in a few years for being able to tie-dye scarves, play lacrosse or program a computer in a language that is already out of date. Mum keeps saying we really must sort something out, and then she's pleased enough that she has said it, like that's as good as sorting it. It drives me mental when she keeps promising something good, like those boots I've been waiting a year for, but it's perfect in this case because I can sleep late and hang out in town.

SECRET: Just between me and my last counsellor (and you if you are hideous enough to be reading someone else's diary – in which case please get your own life and stop right now!!), apparently it is not my mother's failure to pick up the telephone or get in the car with me that is the problem when it comes to organising my life, it's my 'hostile attitude'.

My 'hostile attitude' gets blamed for loads of stuff and lets everyone off the hook, I really don't know what we'd all do without it. The funny thing is that Mum can spend so much time organising trips to the seaside for sick children and supervising activities for teenagers who seem to be *way* happier than me.

I have decided not to dress up for Claire Higgins' end-of-term party tonight. All her friends look *so* exaggerated, like they have to wear every accessory ever invented all at the same time, with shoes as high as most scaffolding, and make-up that wouldn't melt off with a blowtorch. I prefer to go as I am. I'm not out to impress anyone, especially not her lame bunch.

I would love to go to a party where people actually

sat down and talked about real things. Even though I know loads of people I feel really alone, like there's no-one who really gets me.

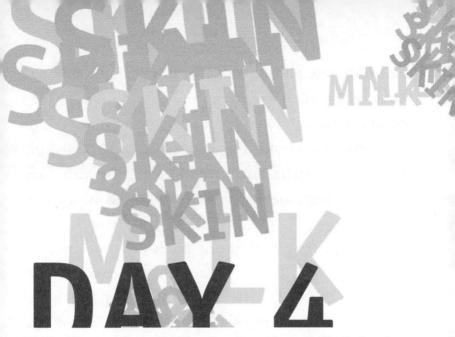

DAY 4

Well, if watching a skin form on hot milk is boring, then Claire Higgins' party was like a *hundred* skins on a *hundred* old mugs of milk. These girls called Aurora and Bianca were ridiculous, all flirty and dancing together and giggling so the guys would all notice them. What's worse is that the guys were such deformities that they actually fell for such an obvious act.

Well, there was *one* nice guy who came into where I was hanging out in the kitchen and he asked me how old I was. I asked him to guess and he said 'fourteen', which pissed me off because he was right, but I think I look older. Anyway he asked me my name, but then Claire walks in and goes 'Oh this is Tia, she's in my class at school,' like as if I couldn't reply on my own. I just felt like I'd been beamed down from some other planet, like everyone else spoke the same language and had the same customs and I was like an ape, an alien ape. I couldn't be bothered talking to him after that.

And then they both went back out to dance to that stupid song that everyone is learning the moves to. I would rather *die* than dance to a song that already had moves. In fact, outside of my bedroom I don't dance at all.

Then when I saw Dee kissing this guy as if she was vacuuming something from his mouth, and Kira playing with her dangly earring in that way that signals that some poor victim is about to be targeted, I called my dad for a lift home. I was really glad I had worn my big sweater as it was kind of cold waiting on the corner, even though it's supposed to be summer already.

As part of the new caring parent thing Dad was all jolly and asked me how it went.

I said 'Fine', and then said, 'Thanks for asking', as my part of the effort. And then because we had both been so amiable we could afford to drive home in silence.

NOTE TO SELF: No more parties. **EVER**.

DAY 5

Went round to Kira's in the morning and Dee was there too. It sounded as if they were already on the twentieth telling of what happened last night, because they were getting really detailed like, 'Did you notice how he looked at me for a split second and then angled his feet in my direction before looking again?' I have to admit I'd missed all these cool signs and signals.

They had decided that I'd failed somehow because I hadn't kissed a guy at the party, and started to lecture me about doing the counting to five hundred thing and asking me why I didn't wear my red dress because it goes so well with my black hair and why I left when it was just getting good.

I wish people would stop telling me how pretty I could look, especially Kira going on about wearing my hair out of my eyes, and Dee having this thing about how I stand, it's like she's been hypnotised by Mrs Traynor. I don't go round telling people what to do with themselves so why can't they just like me as I am? And maybe I didn't kiss anyone because I'm choosy, not because I'm a backward freak ...

When I didn't answer back Kira put on her serious 'goddess' voice and said, 'Your aura has been a little yellow these past few days.' I just stopped myself from saying that I felt the same about her face.

I was in such a pissy mood that I told them I had to go and meet my mum in town, which they know is a lie because I never meet my mum in town, I only ever see her in the kitchen by the microwave, or in front of a TV programme.

Sometimes I feel that Kira and Dee wish I didn't hang out with them. They're probably having a conversation about me right now, but I don't care. All this afternoon I stayed in my room and played loads of songs and danced in front of the full length mirror I nicked from Aidan's room seeing as he's not here to use it. I would *love* an electric guitar, but I know that if I asked for one they'd get it wrong and find me a flute or a cello instead, and I'd be stuck having to get lessons.

I love dancing more than anything and I'm much better than people I've seen at parties; sometimes I wish they could see me dance.

For absolutely no reason I think about Trundle all the time these day. I wish I still had him, I hope his new owners know he prefers beef to chicken. I'm too scared to ask for a new dog in case Dad feels bad again, or in case they get it wrong and get me the dog version of a cello, like a poodle.

Kira called me in the afternoon to check on me, and to tell me she and Dee were meeting the guys from the party whose names I can't remember. She said that she's worried about me and I told her I'm fine. I told her about my plan for tidying and decorating my bedroom and she said great, but she's been hearing it for years so I can't expect excitement.

Mum and Dad were both home before bedtime so we ate a meal. Very good, nice family event. I'd already eaten a bag of crisps earlier but I pretended I was still hungry just in case Mum was going to order Chinese food. Unfortunately she was in an optimistic mood and got three ready-meals from the freezer. I totally understand why we say a prayer before eating

– protection. I made a joke about how maybe Mum should throw out the contents and nuke the box, which didn't go down all that terribly well and now I am in charge of cooking dinner tomorrow night. I called Aidan and he gave me this recipe for fish pie, but I have decided to cook beans on toast or something similar, just so they don't get any ideas about me doing things on a regular basis.

I really miss my chats with Aidan, even though it was usually just ten minutes whenever he came in from somewhere better. Going upstairs without those chats I sort of feel like I haven't spoken to anyone all day, even though I have.

DAY 6

This morning the post arrived after Mum and Dad had left for work. I read my end-of-year report and binned it. I know they won't ask. I used to get really good grades, As and Bs, and now I do really badly. I just can't be bothered. Anyway, don't need to think about it for another six months at least.

Parent-teacher meetings are in the bag. When my folks get the letter from the school asking why they weren't there, I say that I *definitely* told them about it last week. They know they forget about a lot of things when it comes to me and they feel guilty. They say they'll call in and talk to my teachers at some other time, but they never do (luckily for me!)

I think they peaked with my brother Aidan, I'm like

that second Mars Bar when you are full from the first one – OK, but not really worth it.

LATER

Mum and Dad have either

a) found my report in the bin

b) had a phone call

c) heard something on the radio about teenagers

d) decided my frozen pizza pockets for dinner were so bad that I must be evil ...

Or anyway something has made them feel likc making a decision about me.

Now I have three days to come up with a 'constructive and educational' plan for the summer or I am being sent to Aunt Maisie's for six weeks.

Aunt Maisie is a proper aunt, she buys me things, leaves me alone when I need it, doesn't ask awkward questions, talks to me, doesn't boss me about ... did I mention she buys me things?

She is more fun than the rest of us put together and being with her instead of Mum and Dad would be bliss. BUT I couldn't stand to live in the countryside.

Mum says it's not the middle of nowhere (but it is) and that there is plenty to do. There is plenty to do if you are a granny, not if you are a teenager. I do not consider making rag dolls from old socks to be a 'fun activity', even if I did love it when I was seven. Anyway, it doesn't matter, I'm not going. I'm off to talk to Kira's mum, she's a genius at coming up with stuff to get me and Dee off the hook with our folks.

FACT:

DAY 7

FACT: I am now just about angry enough to do something reckless, but too angry to think what that might be. If not even Kira's mum is on my side, then it's safe to say that everyone is against me.

Kira was sitting there too and we were all drinking chamomile tea because they had just read up about it. While Kira's mum said, 'Tia, I think it would be a really good idea for you to get away for a while,' Kira was nodding like she was the wise woman of the west or whatever.

Then they both started this double-attack about me not being happy. Well, show me anyone who is happy! They are not even happy, they've just got more feel-good sayings and CDs than the rest of us. Really.

I called Dee and said that if I can get out of this Aunt Maisie plan then we can both go into town this weekend and hang out at the market stalls and see if we can pretend we are sixteen and get jobs. She said that she was hanging out with Timmy this weekend, except that it took her half an hour to say it because she kept going on about all the cool things he said about her.

I called Aidan and he was out.

INTERESTING INFO: If you get my dad away from my mum you can sometimes encourage him to have an independent thought. But the plan was bigger than the both of us and he said that he and Mum would visit every second weekend, which for some bizarre reason was supposed to make me feel better.

No-one wants me here.

Well FINE!

I will probably be dead in two days anyway from having eaten nothing but cornflakes. I even had to make milk out of yoghurt and water tonight, which doesn't really work.

DAY 8

I'm glad I didn't waste brain cells thinking of anything else to do for the summer, because I just found out that I'm going to Aunt Maisie's anyway. She always comes here so I've never seen her place. Mum tells me it's a large cottage in its own grounds, but if she thinks that will change me into one of those *Pride and Prejudice* girls she's very much mistaken.

I'm sort of relieved though, because I hate everyone right now, but I won't let them know that.

I need to use every minute I have to make it so they won't go into my room while I'm away. That way they can't pull another stunt like the salmon-coloured, flowered wallpaper that appeared when I was off on the weekend school trip to that farm. I am going to push all the mess near the door so it's impossible to get through.

I put all my favourite clothes into a big suitcase and then took them all out again deciding to wash everything first in case she doesn't have a washing machine. I know she will, I just … God, I don't know.

I went around to meet Kira and Dee at the burger place, but they sounded worse than my mother. They kept saying that I'd have a good time and they wish they were going and that I might find a boyfriend there. I told them I don't want a boyfriend, but I didn't say that I didn't want to be all ridiculous like they are over the Timmys. The other guy's name is not actually Timmy I just can't be bothered learning any more names of guys they like, so from now on they are all just Timmy. Once we are all ancient and they get to the altar, then I'll learn the guys' real names.

I didn't even get to say goodbye properly because Dee's brother's friends arrived in, and this needed the girls' full attention in case things don't work out with the current round of Timmys.

I had to ask Dad for money and he said 'How much?' That bugs me because he should really have thought of it and then he should have given me more than I asked for just to make sure I was OK. Instead he gave me exactly what I said and counted it out really carefully like it was a million.

Mum put her head around the door to say goodbye. Then said she had to give me a hug as she wouldn't be seeing me for a couple of weeks, and gave me one of her hugs where there is enough room for two extra people between us, so it's really just her hands on my shoulders and bending a bit to the left.

Trundle used to snuggle up to me and nuzzle my hair with his nose. Aidan gives these big bear hugs, but only when he is coming or going for ages, or on special occasions. He still hasn't called back, which makes me feel like I've lost my only real parent.

I looked up at the sky and wondered what's happened to the stars these days. There are never any when I think to look up. When I was really little and we spent time in Dad's uncle's place by the beach, there were loads of stars. We used to all lie on the beach and Dad would teach us the names of the stars and Mum would get them all muddled up and not on purpose. It was such a laugh, but I haven't explained it very well. It was one of those 'you-had-to-have-been-there' things.

I nearly forgot to pack this diary, good thing it was on top of my jeans with the beads otherwise I would have left it behind. It's weird that I have written more in this than in English class for the last year.

***

I am in bed early.

PRETEND REASON: To get enough sleep to be up bright and early to get to the train in time.

REAL REASON: I am so angry with them that I keep wanting to bite someone's head off whenever either of them says anything, and I don't want to fall out with them just before I go or they might never let me come home.

DAY9

Dad was already in the car so he didn't hear Mrs Traynor go 'coo-eee' over the wall. Seriously, she does that. It's like living next door to someone from a washing powder ad.

'Off on a little trip, dear?' she said with this fake smile.

'Reform school. See you when I'm eighteen.'

And she looked all flustered and scuttled back inside.

Dad stood there with me on the platform until the train came, but I know he was dying to go.

He kept saying, 'Got your ticket?' Then, 'Got your money?'

I even said, yes I had got my raincoat, even though

I don't own one.

I was glad Mum wasn't there so I didn't have to see her smile apologetically at strangers for my ripped black sweater and long black skirt. As if her lace-up brown shoes were not the most disturbing things anyone ever paid money for.

The train ride was fine. I bought some sandwiches from the trolley, but for some reason eating on my own makes me feel really sad, which is why I always do it in front of the TV. I was hungry, but I couldn't eat.

As we were pulling into the station I got a strong feeling that something strange is going to happen during this visit. Not that Kira is right about me being psychic, she just says that to everyone when she wants something out of them, that they are 'psychically attuned'.

Aunt Maisie looks way younger than she must be, and is nothing like my mother, I guess she was the family rebel. She's like one of those older models you see in expensive magazines for elegant country homes. My mum would look ridiculous in jeans, but Aunt Maisie looks better than I do. She's always so stylish. Her hair is now red and to her shoulders, but I know that it could change again by next week.

The station is so small that she could pretty much park on the platform. I don't remember what we talked about first, but once we got to the house she told me that she was really pleased that I had finally agreed to come and visit. That means that I was invited before now and they didn't tell me!

'So, rough few months then?' she sort of half-said and half-asked.

I like that about Aunt Maisie, she gets right to it. She says stuff in two seconds that it would take my mum and dad two centuries to get out of their mouths!

I said, 'Yeah, rough enough,' and she smiled and left it at that.

We had hot crumpets with blackcurrant jam and big cups of tea in the glass conservatory, looking out over the herb garden. I felt so good and relieved just to be somewhere where people weren't against me. I'm sure I won't be serving my full six-week sentence here, but for now it's nice.

Then she said, 'What's your favourite colour?' and I smiled and said, 'Black,' and she said, 'Well, what would be your favourite colour to sleep in?' I thought that was a very Kira and Kira's mum type question, so I said 'Huh?' to buy a little time.

She explained that she'd left off redecorating the room I'm to sleep in, and that we might paint it and it would be ready for tomorrow night. I thought how not being ready for me was just like my mum, but in fact Aunt Maisie had all this amazing stuff done and had waited on purpose so I'd get a colour I liked. I felt more welcome when she showed me the new towels she had bought, and the handmade soaps and the new mirror. The mirror is quite small, but as there is no sound system I won't be dancing in there anyway, so I don't really need a mirror. The room is smaller than my room at home, but because there's nothing thrown on the floor it's *way* bigger in reality. The brass bed is *huge* and there's a soft, light-blue carpet and cotton curtains in the same colour; the window looks out to the back garden.

I don't know what I'll do without being able to shut the door and just put on a track and dance, it's like my version of stress release. But maybe I won't be so stressed here.

Driving to the village we passed this huge field of lavender that looked *amazing* so when we got to the paint shop I chose pale lavender paint. I am now worried that it is close enough to lilac to make me a total hypocrite, but it's not really lilac, it's more of a bluish kind of lavender. Anyway, what's OK for walls is not necessarily OK for wearing outdoors where people can see you.

When we were in the paint shop this almost-ancient man in muddy jeans and a checked shirt came in and started bossing everyone around and not waiting his turn. He ordered twenty tins of Jasmine White and looked as pleased with himself as if he had ordered twenty cars. He must live in a pretty big house, or else he owns a bridge! He was really nasty and reminded me of my geography teacher who shouts because he has a crap haircut and can't get anyone to marry him. (That's my theory anyway.)

We got my room painted pretty fast because of these new spongy roller things and the fact that Aunt Maisie had already covered the carpet and taped the bits near the windows and all that.

Tonight we brought the duvet down to the living room and pulled out the sofa bed so I can sleep here while the paint dries. This is the coolest ever room, with bookcases of old books (duh!, like what else would be on bookcases, Tia?!), statues, leather chairs, a huge writing desk with antique pens, paintings ... all sorts.

I don't know why, but I really feel like crying since yesterday, and I never cry. Wouldn't give them the satisfaction. Once they see you cry they think they are better than you and walk all over you. But I guess it's OK to cry in front of old portraits, and it's just because I'm tired from the journey.

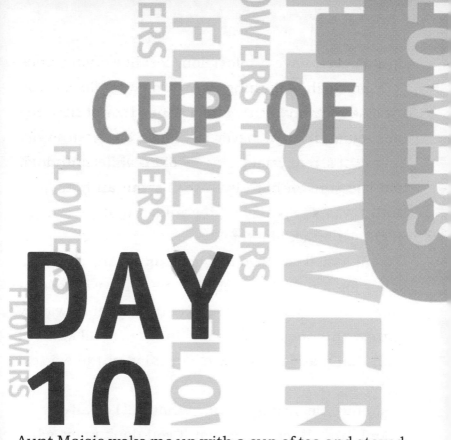

CUP OF FLOWERS

DAY 10

Aunt Maisie woke me up with a cup of tea and stayed chatting while I drank it.

We went to the garden and cut some flowers which I've forgotten the names of already and put them in this vase in my room. It looks great that there is no clutter, just the vase and the mirror.

I spent the afternoon looking through the books but didn't find any that I liked, they were all too old and boring. Even though it is beautiful and all that, I am going to die of boredom here. She doesn't even have a television.

Because I had nothing else to do I went and put all my clothes away neatly and arranged the stuff in the bathroom. I have never had my own bathroom before. It's really modern, tiled in white and gold, and the sunken bath is huge. I spent an hour in it until I was so spongy and wrinkled that I worried I might get stuck like that.

Aunt Maisie is as good a cook as Aidan. We had a salad for lunch, but not like the ones we have at home with tomatoes and cucumber and watery lettuce, this one had so many things in it, all kinds of stuff that made it not taste like salad but like a real meal.

After we cleaned up I said, 'What will I do all day?'

And Aunt Maisie said that if you don't know what to do, it's your job to discover what you should be doing. That is a bit like when Dad says there is no such thing as being bored only being boring, (which is something he should know all about).

So I looked at some books, got more flowers for my room, and refolded my clothes. I saw a TV documentary about a thing called OCD or Obsessive Compulsive Disorder once, where people wash their hands every minute and fold things all day and I hope I don't turn into one while I'm here.

After we finished dinner I just wandered about the garden because I couldn't think what to do. I was too pissed off to even talk to Aunt Maisie or phone anyone, so I cleaned the kitchen, and had another bath (but not in an OCD way).

I wonder if anyone has ever actually *died* of boredom, or if you get so bored that you just lie there and germs take over and you die of that?

DAY 11

In the morning, Aunt Maisie brought me my cup of tea. That really feels good, waking up to someone being nice, not yelling that you will be late and don't use all the hot water and don't eat the bread because it's a bit green.

After breakfast (pancakes! I've never had pancakes for breakfast before) I walked around the garden for a bit and found a bike in the shed. I thought I might as well to go into the village to see if I could buy some magazines. I would not normally ride a bike in case anyone saw me, but no-one lives around here so I knew I was safe enough.

It's a straight road over to the village and on it I cycled past this girl walking a dog who looked about my age (the girl, I have no idea how old the dog was), but I didn't stop. Then when I cycled past her on the way back she waved. I wish I'd stopped to say 'Hi', but what if she was just waving and didn't really want to talk to me?

It was weird, she looked *so* like me, shortish, with blue eyes, pale skin with a few freckles, long straight hair, except she has blonde hair and mine is black. If either one of us dyed our hair we could be twins.

It reminded me of this book that Aunt Maisie used to read to me when I was a little girl, a fairy tale called *Snow White and Rose Red*. I can't remember what happened except it involved two sisters, two princes and one big fish, but I remember I loved it and used to get her to read it to me again and again.

***

LATER

I was going to mention the book to Aunt Maisie at teatime, but was too scared that she wouldn't remember and then I'd feel stupid for saying it and it would be ruined, you know, the idea of it. But then when we were having mugs of hot chocolate at bedtime I did ask, and she knew exactly what I was talking about and went out to her office and came back in with the exact book. She had kept it all this time. I have been reading it over and over to myself in bed and only stopped so I'd get to write in this before falling asleep, which is going to happen any minute now. I had totally forgotten where the fish came into it.

I would love a prince to come along and take me away from all this. Not very likely I know.

DAY12

Today I saw that blonde girl again, this time in the supermarket. I was buying soy milk which is like regular milk, but not from a cow. Aunt Maisie says it's better for you. The girl was wearing a yellow sun-dress and waltzing with the manager in the fruit and veg section. He is an old guy, about seventy, and he was teaching her how to do the steps, and all these old ladies were standing around and loving it and talking about when they used to dance like that in the old days, and what a nice figure the girl had and how they used to have that figure in the old days, and on, and on, and on ... My parents never dance, or at least I have never seen them dance, or touch each other come to think of it.

The girl was humming this waltz music and laughing as he whirled her around. Usually I would think that doing something like that was really pathetic, looking for attention, but she seemed OK.

I have now bought and read every magazine in the village so I'm stuck for what to do for the next week. I thought about taking the train back without a word to anyone, but that would just lead to massive numbers of reasonable discussions, so I know I have to stay here at least until Mum and Dad visit next weekend. Technically it would not be running away as I would be going home, but I won't chance it just yet.

Aunt Maisie caught me sighing on the sofa (she said, 'like a Victorian consumptive', which I think is not good) and asked if I wanted to read the book that was her favourite when she was my age. I thought it would be an adventure thing with boats and pirates, but instead it was a really old and impossible book about a girl who looks a bit ugly if that's her on the front. It's called *Charlotte Brontë*, by Jane Eyre. No. Wait. It's called *Jane Eyre*, and the writer is called Charlotte Brontë. Not that it matters, except to her maybe, and she's dead by now.

In school this year we had to read *Pride and*

Prejudice and it was OK except I couldn't work out who they were talking about because they sometimes said 'Miss Bennett' and it meant one of them and then it meant another sister, and the main girl was called Elizabeth, Liza, Lizzie, Eliza, and a million other names so I got too mixed up. It didn't help that I never actually read the thing, I just watched the film!

I brought *Jane Eyre* up here to my room to keep Aunt Maisie happy, but I won't be reading it.

I am managing to keep the room tidy. Tonight I put some rose petals into my bath and felt like a princess. I think I look more like a witch though, with my long black hair that tangles into a bird's nest five minutes after I've combed it. I wish was more like the Snow White blonde girl I saw in the supermarket. Although we could be twins, she puts herself together better and her expressions and laughing make her prettier. Maybe I look more like Rose Red.

I hope something happens tomorrow. Anything. A TV would be amazing, but not very likely. No wonder people in the countryside claim to have seen aliens. My head will start making stuff up very soon if I don't feed it something.

***

I hate myself. I am ugly and stupid and there is NOTHING good about me. Everyone else has *some* good points. Kira has her meditation and her hippie stuff, Dee is a bit useless too, but at least she looks really good and her brothers and sisters do stuff with her and she laughs a lot. I only ever laugh when Aidan tells me stories about his friends in the band, about when they make mistakes on stage. I laugh at some TV shows too, but never when there is someone else in the room.

Things I HATE

my hair
my body
my face
my brain
my voice
my family
my friends
my school
my whole life

I know that I was an accident and my parents probably wish I'd never been born.

* * *

When I was sitting in the front room I saw that horrible man from the paint shop arguing with a man with a van. I don't think they had an accident because both the van and the car looked fine, so it doesn't make sense why they stopped there to yell at each other. Maybe they hate life too.

* * *

LATER

Aunt Maisie could tell I was in a vile mood from how I just sat there biting my nails. She asked me how that *Jane Eyre* novel was going and I told her it was too difficult. So she had me bring it back down and said to read one line from anywhere. It's a pain when she gets all teacher-y but it's always over fairly quickly. Anyway, I read a sentence from the book and she asked if I understood that sentence, and I said 'Yes', because it took a little bit of thinking about but was easy enough. Then she said to do it again with another line from anywhere and I did it and it was pretty easy too. I guess I was just put off because it was so big and old and lacking in pirates.

I read the first few pages in the bath and it is a bit depressing; it's all about this little girl who people say is bad, but really she hasn't done anything wrong, everyone's just out to get her, so I could *totally* relate. She also reads this book about birds and about sea fowl, which I think are seagulls, at least I don't know what else they could be as there are no such things as sea chickens. I used to be really into garden birds, but I would die if anyone knew that now.

There is a chaffinch who lives in the tree outside this bedroom.

Aunt Maisie says we can go for a long drive tomorrow so I can see the countryside. It's hard to get excited about cows, but it will be great to be out of the house. I think she is trying to make sure I don't get more pissed off with the world before she has to hand me back!

HILARIOUS
FISH-PASTE SANDWICHE
BLUEBERRY

DAY 13

It was hilarious, we packed a picnic and everything. The people I know back home would laugh themselves into a coma if they heard about someone going on a picnic with their aunt with fish-paste sandwiches and blueberry muffins.

We drove to an old ruined castle which was very cool. Aunt Maisie wanted to take pictures of it, so I wandered around for a couple of hours and was imagining that I was Rose Red from the fairy tale and married to my prince. There was no-one there because of it being a weekday so I could be as loopy as I wanted.

Then we went to this place that has a waterfall and that's where we ate the picnic and then walked in the woods for a bit. On the way back I fell asleep in the car and now I am going to read a couple of pages of *Jane Eyre*.

It's funny, but if someone told me that I would have to do all that for a day I would think I would despise it and do whatever it took to get out of it. But I actually (I have to admit) had fun.

I called Mum and Dad and they had nothing to say except that everything was fine, and I just said the same, 'Fine', as if the day would be ruined if I told them about it. Also, I want them to worry about me a bit for a change or at least wonder how I really am.

I know people make phone calls about me when I am not there so I hope Aunt Maisie is telling them that I am damaged from all the abandonment. But then my mum would just tell her to make me do the weeds in the garden like she does at home if she catches me moping. She calls it moping, but I call it feeling hurt, and pulling weeds has never done much for it.

DAY 14

Aunt Maisie was going into the village to get her nails and hair done, and asked me did I want a lift. She dropped me off on the main street and I told her I'd see her back at the house sooner or later. It's about a thirty minute walk, which is fine when all you have to do in the day is chop fruit and read an old book. I mean it's not like someone famous will drop by and I'll miss them.

I saw the man who bought all the paint and did the yelling at the man, coming out of the bank, so I crossed the road to avoid him. As soon as I got to the other side I ran straight into that blonde girl, and she had a crazy sandy-coloured dog that was dragging her along the street, the same one as the first time I saw her. The dog came right over and started jumping up on me and she was saying, 'Really Buddy, have you no manners?' as if the dog spoke perfect English.

I said, 'It's OK, I like dogs.'

She told me she was taking it out for this old couple because the man had hurt his leg in a fall and his wife was too busy fussing to be able to walk the dog.

Then she said, 'Come on then', and at first I thought she was talking to the dog until she laughed and said, 'Well, it's not like there's anything better to do around here! I'm Jenny.'

I said 'Tia.' (I am very relieved about my name as I know it was almost Mary after my mum.)

I know it sounds weird, but it was like we'd both decided to be friends already.Maybe it's easier to make friends here than back home. Less politics.

The old couple tried to get us to come in, but Jenny obviously didn't want to and I didn't either so she said that she was showing me around. She probably had a bad experience with their tea and fruitcake before.

Jenny is fifteen (like I will be in ten weeks) and is the most smiley, happy person I have ever met. Kira would say she was probably a game show hostess in a past life. I think in a past life I was probably someone who lived in the woods and ate mice.

After talking to Jenny I now know for sure that there is nothing to do here, not even a swimming pool, or an outdoor market, or a cinema or any more people our age.

'Except for Jackson. He's a year older than us, and by the look of you, I don't reckon you'd think much of him.'

I have no idea what she meant by that, but she didn't say it in a bitchy way so she wasn't being mean. In fact she is so sunny and happy that I can't imagine her ever being mean or sarcastic. I was almost too freaked to say anything in case I sounded too negative. Anyway it was cool because she was really comfortable with chatting away, a bit like people who have been prisoners for weeks and then they get to talk to the press and keep going on for hours.

'I've known Jackson forever because we both get sent here for the summer, but he has to work for his grandfather most of the time, giving tours of the Big House or doing repairs or odd jobs, so I usually don't see him much. I spend most of the summer with my mum's old nanny, Nanny Gloria, and she keeps me busy running errands for neighbours.'

Jenny asked me if I had seen the Park yet and I thought it was beyond weird to have a park in the middle of the countryside, where it would be just more fields and trees in the middle of fields and trees.

It only took about twenty minutes and we arrived at this place that was the best I have ever seen in my ENTIRE LIFE. It's *enormous* with this huge lake, and it's not flat, but not really hilly, and there are different trees in like 'designer clumps', and the most amazing stately home in the distance. Jackson *lives* there, in what they call the Big House, with his grandfather. That made me laugh because it seemed *so* not normal. A place like that is for visiting with the school, not for living in! Anyway we didn't get to go that far because Nanny Gloria lives in the Gate Lodge.

Jenny's bedroom is excellent. It has a four-poster bed with cushions and pillows in every colour. There's an old tin bath on the floor at the end of it that is stuffed full of dolls and soft toys that she's had since she was a baby. We just hung out and talked loads. Usually it takes me ages to get to know a new person so it was weird, but nice.

It took me forever to walk back to Aunt Maisie's, so from now on I will take the bike with me.

I'm at a really sad bit in *Jane Eyre* where she's sent away to this school where she is freezing all the time and she is made out to be really bad, and she has never done anything wrong except defend herself against the family she was living with. It makes me feel really good about having a warm bed and food to eat. Even my room at home and things like cornflakes would be a luxury to her. Every couple of pages there's a word like 'subjoined' or 'ottoman' that I don't get, but I still understand what it all means anyway. I hope it gets happy soon.

DAY 15

Today was another not-boring day.

I cycled around to the Gate Lodge as I told Jenny I would, and we spent the morning learning to bake bread (not that I will ever admit that to anyone in the free world). Nanny Gloria is exactly as you would expect a nanny to be, really no-nonsense and with smiley eyes even when she is pretending to be cross. We made olive bread and tomato bread and I took some back to Aunt Maisie when I went back for lunch.

Then in the afternoon Jenny came over here and we sat in the garden on the sun loungers and talked about our families and friends back home and school and all that. God, we could almost swap lives at this point, we know so much about each other.

Jenny goes to boarding school because her dad is a diplomat and so her parents have to travel all around the world all the time. She used to go with them, but then she saw a film set in a boarding school and begged her parents to let her go to one. She said she just got tired of leaving her friends behind and having to make new ones every few years whenever her dad was posted somewhere new.

She was laughing so hard when I told her about the state of my bedroom back home, and said that at her school it was three girls to a room and you had to keep it immaculate. Then just so she didn't think I was a complete degenerate, I showed her my room here, to prove I could keep a place nicely.

For some reason we ended up talking about dogs and I told her about how I did have a dog once, for a few weeks and that I really missed him.

I didn't go into how Mum got annoyed when Trundle chewed her bag from work, and how she then mysteriously developed an allergy to dogs (an allergy that had no symptoms whatsoever!) and she got Dad to give him away. I didn't speak to either of them for a week after that and Mum said it was a good lesson in selflessness and Dad just looked really upset. She did buy me a new bag to break my silence, but it's hardly the same thing.

Jenny has so many goals, she wants to play hockey for a national team, she wants to be really good at oil painting and to earn enough money to buy her own apartment before she is twenty. I only ever want to get through the day without spilling something on my clothes so I don't have to do too much laundry. I wish I had something that I *really* wanted to do, like when I used to run out to that tyre-swing Aidan made for me years ago at the beach place.

DAY 16

Well, Jenny was right, I *don't* think much of Jackson. He is so full of himself and *really* pushy, like all the worst guys I have ever met glued together and given a posh voice. I was really hoping he'd be nice and that I might even end up really liking him and going out with him.

STORY OF MEETING JACKSON:

I cycled up to see Jenny but there was no-one in, and I remembered she'd said that she and Nanny Gloria would be shopping for people in the morning. So I left my bike there and walked up to the Big House. Aunt Maisie had told me that no-one lives in the bottom rooms of the Big House and that tour parties can book to go around them. I just wanted to look in one of the windows to see what it looked like, whether it was like in a fairy tale or like in a museum.

Walking up the wide stone steps and across the courtyard I pretended that the building was mine and I was a lady, or a baroness or duchess, or whatever you call the type of woman who lives in a place like this.

I peered through the glass into one of the darkened rooms and could make out a chandelier, some beautiful chairs, and a fireplace with a huge oil painting over it. I imagined myself sitting by the fire, wearing a long dress, reading *Jane Eyre*, as if I always read important books.

Right at that moment this guy (who I knew must be Jackson) appeared beside me and without saying hello, or asking who I was, said sharply, 'You shouldn't be here! You have to go!' And he took my arm and started leading me away.

I pulled my arm back and told him where he could go, using the kind of language that usually gets me in trouble. I quickly walked back down the steps and out of the Park and rode home so furious at him. For God's sake, I was just looking!!

It was like he was some big lord of the manor and I was some poor wench who would steal the family silver. Well, I'm glad Jenny doesn't hang out with him much.

I went back to Aunt Maisie's and read in the garden.

I am going to go back tonight and look around. I bet it looks really amazing at night and there will be less chance of that stupid Jackson seeing me. He is like this monster of a man in *Jane Eyre* who owns the house she has gone to work in as a governess. In the book Mr Rochester throws his weight around just because he owns the estate, and Jackson is *exactly* like that and he doesn't even own the place, his grandfather does.

After dinner I told Aunt Maisie I was going out to ride my bike to Jenny's (which is true as I'll leave my bike there) and would be back before ten. It was really dark apart from the lights on the bike, and so quiet, not even a car anywhere near. The sound of the tyres on the road and my own breathing were all I could hear. An owl hooted once and I stopped to work out where it was, but it didn't make another sound. When I got to the Gate Lodge I saw that the Park gates were locked, so I just had to turn back. I would love to see the Big House at night, I bet Jenny knows a way to get in. It's a pity that such a magical place can be so wasted on a guy like Jackson.

If I lived there I would light up the courtyard and dance there every night to the sound of violins and an owl hooting in the far distance. I'd wear a floaty dress and amazing shoes and do all these ballroom dances with a charming duke, or at least a guy who doesn't make me want to throw up.

DAY 17

Weird. Jenny called around in the morning and she had been speaking to Jackson. He had dropped in to her place at breakfast time, and asked about who I was (probably wanted to run me out of the country entirely!). Jenny said that I was her friend and he had better be nice to me.

Jenny tried to explain his mean, bossy behaviour away. Apparently, his grandfather is sick and he (Jackson) told Jenny that yesterday he had to get me to leave the courtyard because his grandfather was coming, and that his grandfather would have shouted at me and been really horrible and banned me from the place forever, because since his illness he does things like that. I told her that Jackson himself had done a good enough job of being rude and horrible, and was the biggest mistake of a person I had ever met. She tried to stick up for him, but I know that's just because she is nice about everyone. She stayed for lunch and then had to go.

* * *

HOLD TIGHT FOR THE FREAKY WEIRD BIT: Some time during the afternoon, without me or Aunt Maisie noticing, a big bunch of lavender with a note attached was left on the front doorstep. The note said,

Dear Tia,

Although it was not the best start, I am really looking forward to getting to know you this summer.

Yours, Jackson F.

Aunt Maisie always thinks that something is more of a big deal than it is because she is a bit dramatic, and sure enough her eyebrows were way up around the top of her head.

'Must have made an impression!' she said in a mysterious voice.

I know *exactly* what sort of impression I made, so I think that he must have a thing for Jenny and after their conversation he wants to keep her happy by staying on my good side. Or else he thinks I am properly crazy and wants to make sure I don't throw bricks through his windows. He can forget about meeting me again, I'm not going to let some bully from the Big House tell me what to do.

We went grocery shopping and I cooked a vegetarian lasagne all by myself out of a recipe book and it turned out really well. I can't wait to tell Aidan. I wonder does he even know where I am?

I called Dee, but she didn't ask about me, she just talked about her stuff like as if I wouldn't be doing anything. So after ten minutes I said I had to go. She said that Daniel, the guy from the party was asking about where I had got to. I think she's making it up to make it sound like I'm missing something.

DAY 18

I have decided I need a goal. I can't think of one yet, but I know it will have nothing whatsoever to do with hockey or maths.

I bet if I had a goal people would like me more and think I was doing something important. Then I could talk about what I was doing and not just about how crap everything is. I know I say that I don't like most people, and it's a bit true because everyone annoys me, but I would love some friends to be happy with. Jenny is so happy already that I don't think I could ever catch up, but I will ask her to help me get a goal.

First I will read ten pages of *Jane Eyre* in case there is some inspiration in there. I am loving reading it, but reading classic books isn't really a goal because I'm already doing it

***

OK, done the ten pages. I now know that my goal will not involve sketching or governessing.

LATER

Went to Jenny's and Jackson was there. It was like when a well-behaved dog and a cat meet. Me and Jackson hated each other straight away.

He looked at me for a long time and said, 'Do you always wear black?'

'Do you *always* ask stupid questions?' I fired back

Then Jenny got all bright and breezy and told us we all had to get along or we'd end up having to hang out with old people all summer.

She was right, so we pretended to be friendly. He offered to make me a cup of chamomile tea, and I said that the lavender he left me is very nice. I didn't tell him how amazing it looks in the pink glass bowl I put it in, or how it makes the whole room smell delicious. I didn't want him thinking I thought he was great or anything just for picking some flowers that were obviously meant to impress Jenny and not me.

I accepted his apology about the other day in the courtyard, because apparently his grandfather really has good and lost it, and might have done anything if he saw me there looking through the window. Jenny says he is a lovely old man, and it's a shame that since he was sick he doesn't really know what's going on, and that when he gets afraid he shouts.

Jackson so fancies Jenny, it's really obvious. He doesn't really look at me or speak to me as he is so focused on her. He's *so* not my type anyway, dressed in a rugby shirt and pristine jeans, with sun bleached hair and a posh accent. Also, he talked about things that had nothing to do with me and I think that's just rude.

Also, he complains a lot. The next thing he said was, 'Something is going on with Mr Walsh and I can't work out what it is.'

'Mr Walsh is the estate manager,' Jenny explained.

'It's like since Grandad's illness, Mr Walsh thinks the place is his, and any time I ask questions or ask if I can see the accounts, he treats me like I'm some interfering kid who has no right being there.'

I decided that this Mr Walsh has the right idea about how to treat Jackson. I might try treating him like an itrritating kid myself! He has this annoying habit of swaying when he talks, backwards and forwards with his hands deep in his pockets. Give him a pipe and he could be someone's Dad. I have never, ever met someone my age who is so un-hip. I mean, there's Dolores from the year below me with the glasses thicker than a cake, but apart from her.

They talked about Mr Walsh for a while and I was half tuned-out. Then when Jackson said something about Mr Walsh buying paint and hiring people to paint the east wing, I realised he might be that man I'd seen in the village.

'I know him, he wears a checked shirt and bought twenty pots of Jasmine White emulsion.'

'Ten', Jackson said.

'No, twenty,' I insisted, 'I remember because our house is number 20.'

'It only takes ten,' he mumbled. 'I know because we did the exact same thing four years ago. I wonder why he bought so much extra?'

This thought made Jackson go all quiet and fidgety so Jenny said, 'Why don't we go for a walk to the lavender field?'

The Park is huge. Enormous. We walked for ages, past the lake, then past the Big House and a cute little fancy stone hut thing, and then through the lavender field (even bigger than the one you can see on the way to the village) and on to a funny looking single storey building which Jenny said was the old tearooms.

'They used to serve afternoon tea here, and have dances, but it's been closed down for over thirty years,' Jackson explained.

Then they both began to talk about when they were little and would play together for the summer. The abandoned tearoom was their favourite place to play until three summers ago Mr Walsh decided it was dangerous and locked the place up entirely. They didn't fight it because it was the same summer that Jackson had to start learning about the estate and Nanny Gloria got Jenny started with the good citizen bit.

The tearoom is about the size of six classrooms, and has amazing doors, ceilings, and windows, but it's really dirty and run down. It was a single huge space like a nightclub, but a daytime, old-fashioned one, with chairs and tables stacked at the sides. We didn't go in because Jenny once saw a rat there, which Jackson said was a mouse. I wasn't in the mood for either.

As we headed back through the lavender field it suddenly began to rain. So we ran back to the tearoom, but the doors were locked. For a second I thought about kicking in the door and getting in that way, but I knew it would look bad. I had to do something because the rain was now getting quite heavy. Luckily, there was a window with no glass that was pretty high up, but big enough to get through. I had Jackson give me a leg up and I got through and jumped down the other side. Then it was easy to unbolt the door and let them in from the inside.

I didn't tell them about how we used to break into the school gym during the holidays, and how I always went first because I'm so small. I didn't want them to think I was a total vandal.

Once we were all inside there wasn't much to do except stand there and say obvious things like, 'Look at that rain!'

After twenty minutes or so it was still bucketing down and we knew we'd be there for a while at least. Jenny started to show Jackson how to waltz like the manager of the supermarket had showed her, and we both nearly fell over with shock when he just took off waltzing with her. He dances better than most professionals.

'We have to learn it in school,' he shrugged, suddenly embarrassed. I actually though it was so cool, but I didn't tell him that. Imagine someone as annoying as him actually being able to do something good.

He then looked at me as if he felt he had to dance with me too, so I quickly started looking around and commenting on the walls and mirrors and chairs. I don't know why, but I was suddenly really aware of my clumpy black boots compared to Jenny's cute, red shoes. I'd have been like a bloody elephant. I can't do those kind of dances, only the kind where you dance by yourself to rock music, preferably totally alone. I'd love to be able to dance like Jackson, but it's not likely.

The rain went on for ages and we cooked up this plan for cleaning and tidying the place so we'd have somewhere to hang out.

Jackson was *so* psyched about the idea because he sleeps in a dorm at boarding school (like Jenny), then in the Big House he's at his grandad's beck and call, and in his parents' house his little brother is always coming into his room. There is something so unattractive about a guy getting overly-excited. I much prefer guys who play it cool and act like they don't care about anything. Suddenly he was a geek again.

He walked us back to the Gate Lodge, no doubt hoping for time alone with Jenny, poor girl. I got on my bike so I don't know how successful he was with the whole Jenny thing.

***

Aunt Maisie showed me some recipes for oatmeal cookies that keep fresh for days in a tin. It took me a while, but I managed to make two batches of them. I made the normal ones first and then got carried away because they actually tasted like cookies and not like something that I'd made. In the next lot I put raisins in and these ones taste even better. I am now totally in love with myself and think I am the best cook in the world! I put them in a cool red tin Aunt Maisie gave me, and we'll keep them in the tearoom for snacks.

Aunt Maisie laughed at the way I only let us have one cookie each with our hot chocolate.

I read more *Jane Eyre* and realised that no-one is really into cooking in that book, because they leave it all up to the kitchen staff. Maybe Mr Rochester wouldn't drink so much wine if Jane made him the odd oatmeal and raisin cookie. Actually, she'd be better off just leaving, I don't think he really wants her around. If a man acts weird it's not the girl's job to fix him as if he was a shirt with a rip in it.

I have been having loads of dreams about flowers and food all in a big messy pile, and people fighting me, trying to take it all away. I bet I have another of those dreams tonight. I bet Kira would know what it means, she has a book about dream interpretation.

Tomorrow I am going to work really hard all day at getting the tearoom in order and then I will be able to sit in there and look out over the lavender and think about my goal.

DAY 19

Aunt Maisie still wakes me up with a cup of tea every morning and I really love that. It makes me feel like a lot of stuff from home is getting fixed, like I am getting enough attention for now and for then.

I got the leftover blue lavender paint and two brushes and put them in a bag along with the tin of oatmeal cookies.

Jackson and Jenny were already sweeping when I got there, and I got busy so that they get that I am serious about this. I know back home I am really lazy, but that's just because there is nothing I want to do. Here I want to do things even if I don't know what they are.

Jackson said, 'That colour really suits you', and I

just gave him a look because I was all in black as usual so I guessed he was being sarcastic. I bet he was just trying to sound all charming in front of Jenny. But about an hour later I caught my reflection in a newly-washed window and saw that I had got a big streak of lavender paint on the side of my face from when I opened the can to see how much was in there. There was some on my hand too, so I must have touched my face and it wiped off. It least I didn't pick my nose and leave that all painty, but still I felt as big an idiot as that time I sat on a chewing gum paper and had it stuck to my arse for a full day in town. Dee swore she didn't see it but Kira told me in a game of truth or dare that she did and that everyone told each other not to tell me.

Anyway, I was feeling embarrassed and didn't talk to Jackson much after that, I just pretended I was too busy to notice when he said something funny or asked a question. Even when we stopped for a half-dozen cookie-breaks, I made myself all distant, and said I was 'tired' or 'thinking' whenever Jenny asked. A guy would never ask you how you are feeling unless you had trained him really well.

It was amazing now much we got done. The floor was spotless, the chairs, tables and windows washed, and we'd made a start on stripping off the old peeling paintwork on the wooden window frames. We were just deciding how much of the room to paint in lavender, when Mr Walsh rushed in. He had a look on his face like he'd eaten a vat of chillies, his mouth open and a red fire in his cheeks.

He was so obviously trying to sound in control, but not really doing that great a job when he roared, 'What is going *on* here?'

Jackson didn't even look at him and said really calmly, 'We are cleaning this place up because Bob and I have decided we want to hang out here this summer. Grandfather is fine with it, and it's his tearoom, no-one else's.'

I had no idea who Bob was, and thought that the idea of Jackson having an imaginary friend at his age made him seem so much more interesting.

'Your grandfather hasn't the capacity to make those sorts of decisions,' Mr Walsh was practically spitting by now.

Jackson answered, still calm, 'Well, then I'll ask my uncle, after all he's the heir. In fact, he'll be here briefly tomorrow evening and I'll ask him then. Will you be wanting to meet with him, Mr Walsh?'

Mr Walsh just made a face and walked away. He is

so rude, I've never met anyone like him. Oh, except I said that about Jackson who turned out to be more sappy than awful.

'You can't just set up camp anywhere you want. This Park is a business,' Mr Walsh shouted from half way across the lavender field.

'And a home, and at least for the summer it's my home,' Jackson boomed back, sounding like Mr In-Charge.

I didn't know he had it in him!

Mr Walsh had been way too angry for what was going on. After all, the place had been locked up for years. I wonder if he bought the extra paint so he could do the tearoom up by himself? And then sit there drinking tiny china cups of earl grey tea all day and letting the Park and Big House crumble to the ground!

It was after 6p.m., and we couldn't believe we'd been working for *seven hours* with only cookie breaks. We decided to leave the painting for another day, that way (as Jenny and Jackson agreed) Bob could help too. I wanted to ask them who Bob was, but it was kind of hard to do as I couldn't work out how to stop cold-shouldering Jackson without it seeming odd.

Luckily, us girls had already made plans to watch a movie in Jenny's bedroom.

Jackson looked a bit sad that we didn't invite him, but when we explained it was a girls' night in, he looked relieved not to be involved, and practically ran off.

Once he'd gone I could get the info that Bob is Jackson's cousin who is seventeen and hasn't been over for the last four summers. Apparently he is short, loud and annoying and keeps doing silly things like tipping food into people's laps or making fart sounds under his armpit to get attention. Jenny says that she hopes his last four years have made him understand that something is only funny when both people are laughing. Then, because she always has to see the good side, she said she's sure he is very changed and will be fine to hang out with.

'Yes Jenny, maybe he's grown a foot taller and been in a Swiss finishing school for the last four years, majoring in the social graces.'

'Anyway, if he's completely unbearable we can gang up on him and throw him in the lake,' she said miserably, which means that he must be pretty hideous.

While Jenny and I sat there getting toast crumbs

on her bed I somehow told Jenny that I was really jealous of the way that she dresses and laughs, and the way she is so whirling and happy. Then I was amazed when she told me that she was really jealous of the way I say funny things, and the way I am so daring, like I don't let other people dictate my life. We agreed to help each other, and Jenny said she will nudge me whenever I start to look miserable so I can remember to smile. And I am going to encourage her every time she says or does something daring, something that is not meant to make someone else happy.

I feel really good after that chat and I think that Jenny is now my best friend, even though I don't know her for nearly as long as I know Kira and Dee. I think sometimes you just click with people, and it doesn't matter how long or short a time you've known them.

Nanny Gloria let us bring the TV and dvd player up to Jenny's room and we watched this really old movie where the man and the woman were fighting all the time, but it was as if, each time they danced together, they fell in love in spite of themselves. The man wasn't my type, probably not anyone's type, all skinny and a pointy chin, but when he was dancing you thought he was really handsome. It was brilliant.

I had to cycle quickly because I was quite late because we were having such a laugh afterwards, acting out the scenes from the movie.

Aunt Maisie said that my mum called and said they won't be visiting this weekend as planned, but that she asked did I need anything.

'Parents, I need parents,' I mumbled, and made my way upstairs.

I am not sure if I am now in a good mood or a bad mood.

DAY20

I'm going to be the best dancer in the world. That is my goal. No up-to-date stuff either, only the romantic dances like that lady in the movie last night. The trouble is that I need someone to teach me, and someone to dance with.

I wonder if you can do that for a career, dancing like they did in the olden days?

'Hello, I'm a doctor', 'Hello, I'm a lawyer', 'Hello, I'm a long-dress-type dancer, like in black and white films.'

I practised waltzing around the garden because Aunt Maisie was out for the morning. Sometimes I did it as Rose Red, sometimes as the girl in the film last night, and sometimes as me. I wish I could get it right, I know that there is complicated stuff you can do that looks better. Problem is that if I ask Jackson to help me then he will think he is great and that I fancy him. So I'll maybe go to the supermarket at a quiet time and see if the manager is free (joke!).

This afternoon when I was walking past the lake on the way to the tearoom, Jackson was standing there (in a *very* unfortunate pair of loafers) as if he was waiting, and when he saw me said he had a surprise. I guessed he had got something for Jenny and wanted to see if I thought she'd like it. Instead of going to the tearoom we turned towards the little hut. It's tiny, about the size of an ordinary garden shed, but it's a hexagon shape and made of stone. Inside it also has loads of flowers and angels and seashells carved on the stone and a bench that runs right around the edge. The door is the best. It's made of wood and has iron fancy bits that look like ivy all over it. Anyway it was totally empty except for a cardboard box with a grey baby rabbit inside. Jackson seemed at a bit of a loss for how to explain it.

'I caught these kids trying to put it in the lake to see if it could swim. And when I yelled they just ran off and left it there on the bank. I've been feeding him water and grass, but I don't really know what to do. Jenny is usually the one who's good in these situations.'

Suddenly I wanted to prove to Jackson that I was every bit as caring as Jenny so I scooped up the rabbit (luckily it let me and didn't bite me or anything!) and fed it one of the carrots Jackson had put on the bench.

'It'll be too dangerous around here for the poor little thing, what with foxes and dogs, so you'll need to keep him in your bedroom,' I said.

'I'll need to sneak the box past Mr Walsh and Grandfather.'

'Or just keep him in your pocket and make him a bed from a t-shirt once you're in there. Is your grandfather hard of hearing by any chance?'

'Completely deaf. This morning I asked him what he wanted for breakfast, and he answered that I was under no circumstances to swim until the weather got warmer. His nurse says you have to shout right up close if you want him to hear.'

'Great, then he won't hear this little thing scratching about.'

Jenny has no such hearing problems, and she heard us talking while on her way to the tearoom and came over to the hut. She squealed a lot when she saw the baby rabbit and asked what its name was. And because Jackson is in love with her he asked her to name it, so now it is called Cutie-Pie, or just Pie for short, and travels around in the large front pocket of Jackson's jacket.

We needed some soft things to sit on, to make the tearoom more comfortable for hanging around in. The plan was that we would all go up to the Big House and then Jenny and I would wait on the lawn below Jackson's bedroom window and catch blankets and pillows as he threw them down.

They were not blankets and pillows like in any other house, but really heavy and fancy throws and velvet embroidered cushions.

'Good catch Jenny,' Jackson shouted from above and I remembered his grandfather is deaf so we could do that.

'Thanks,' she yelled back as he ducked back in to fetch more.

I wanted to yell, 'Bum!', or something much worse, as loud as I could because it would have been so out of keeping with where we were, but I remembered my goal to be a great dancer and great dancers don't do things like that.

I don't know why, but I suddenly blurted out, 'You don't have a thing for Jackson do you?'

'God, no!' Jenny said.

I was very pleased to hear that. There's no way I could hang out with them if they got together, they are sappy enough as friends, both so nice all the time. Imagine if they got all loved-up as well!

One of the pillows had gone flying so I went to fetch it back to the pile and saw Mr Walsh in the distance. He seemed to be on his knees at the door of the fancy hut (I bet there's a proper word for it, I must ask Aunt Maisie.)

I have worked out what is wrong with Jackson, he is too polite and formal even when he is very relaxed. He also has no pride for being so obvious about Jenny when she isn't into him. Also, he doesn't care that he isn't cool in *any* way. Also, there are other things that I haven't got exactly the right way of describing yet.

We spent the rest of the day in the tearoom, hanging out, doing a bit of arranging and also fussing over Cutie-Pie. Mr Walsh came past, but as soon as he saw us he turned around and back across the lavender field.

'That man is up to something,' Jackson said.

'Definitely,' we agreed. And it felt like we were better friends because we all didn't like Mr Walsh.

Just as we were finishing the last bits, someone else arrived.

At first Jenny and I didn't have a clue who it was. He was very tall, basketball-player tall, and had brown curly hair that sort of flopped into his eyes. He dressed in the same style as Jackson, way-too-old-gentleman-sportsmen-go-casual, jeans and a golf shirt turned up at the collar. Jenny suddenly said, 'Oh my God,' and looked like she was about to pass out.

It all became clear when Jackson said, 'Bob, you remember Jenny don't you?'

Bob seemed equally shocked and asked Jenny where her braces had gone. He kept staring at her like he couldn't believe his eyes.

Today is the sad day that our good friend Jenny officially turned into GOOP. This is the most exact word to describe how she lost the run of herself the second Bob started talking to her. She usually giggles at what you say, but she usually waits until you've said it. She has also now developed this habit of pushing back her hair even if it is already pushed back. When Dee and Kira get like this it really annoys me, but with Jenny it is so sweet. He had better fall for her, that's all I can say, even if it does break Jackson's heart.

Jackson whispered, 'No more coffee for Jenny,' to me, as we all tackled the very last bit of paint stripping together. Bob and Jenny got nothing done; they were talking at a machine-gun pace about God knows what. What I like about Jackson is that he is calm.

It's weird to think that one day Bob will be the owner of the Park and the Big House and the tearoom. 'Bob' is not the name of a person who is going to be lord of a manor, or squire or whatever the term is. Bob is a name for a guy who lifts things for a living. It's a perfectly good name, just not if you know how to tie your own cravat. He's probably called Robert Lionel Jeremy Forsythe and is just going through a phase. I bet his mum never calls him Bob. God, what is with me and guys' names? Like I convict them before we've even got to know each other. I'll give him a chance. After all, Jackson turned out not to be so bad.

Anyway, Bob thought it was hilarious to have a rabbit called Pie, even when we explained that it was short for Cutie-Pie and not some sick joke about us having a plan to eat him.

I stayed up late and made flapjacks and the ones towards the middle of the pan taste great.

EMBARRASS

DAY21

The phrase for today is *MAXIMUM EMBARRASSMENT*. I wished that the ground would open up and swallow me, even then it would just spit me out for being such an idiot. I was waltzing around the garden again this morning and suddenly Jackson appeared, right there, beside the roses. I HATE how he does that, he's like a ghost or something. I was mortified and so angry that he had just walked around the back instead of ringing the doorbell.

'We *do* have a doorbell you know,' I said in a really pissy voice.

'Yeah, I know,' he said, 'I've been ringing it for ages.'

I asked him what did he want and he laughed and said that he had decided that I'm not so tough so I could switch it off. God, that is *so* arrogant, like he thinks he can just do and say what he wants and I'll be OK with it.

Then he said, 'Look, Tia, if you want to learn to dance, I can show you.'

And because it is my goal and a goal is a thing that you make massive sacrifices for, I let him show me how to do a waltz. It was horrible at first, and I got really self-conscious about doing it right and then I was thinking what if my hands got really sweaty or if I fell over and took him with me. None of that happened, I just learned how to do some steps without looking at my feet. I was doing it all wrong before, so I suppose it's good to know the real steps now. The first thing is that I have to hold my arms right, and be down with my knees bent for the first step and then up on my toes for the next two. Also I have to let the man decide where we are going (which would not work in real life because my dad can't make a decision and we would end up homeless and starving if my mum wasn't in charge).

I was wearing my big boots and he said to take them off and I was suddenly really worried in case my socks had loads of holes in them, or smelled awful or something, but they didn't, thank God, and after about half an hour I was too knackered to carry on so we went inside. I made some fresh iced tea the way Aunt Maisie had showed me and found a carrot for Pie, who had been in Jackson's pocket all the time, but I had kept Jackson dancing at a bit of a distance so I hadn't noticed. Apparently rabbits don't get dizzy.

I remembered what he said about me being not so tough, so I asked him what he meant by that. He made me promise not to have a big reaction and then said,

'Well, you look all dangerous with your hair in your eyes and your black clothes – not that there's anything wrong with them, you always look stylish just it's always dark and edgy. Then you always say something that pushes people away from knowing more about you, even if it is usually quite funny.'

'*Very* funny,' I corrected him.

'You see,' he laughed, 'Totally defensive.'

Then I couldn't say I wasn't defensive because that would be defensive, so I couldn't win.

'So I decided,' he continued, 'That you are like a little yapping dog, all bark and no bite.'

I didn't know whether to laugh or cry, I felt really noticed or something. For once I couldn't think of a single smart-alec thing to say, so I drank some more iced tea and asked where Jenny was. She was pretending to be sick so she wouldn't have to go to a community lunch that Nanny Gloria was running in the village.

'And Bob?'

'Back at the house, trying to have a conversation with Grandfather. I really ought to go and rescue him.'

You see, that annoys me. No-one says 'ought' except in *Jane Eyre* (which I haven't read in a couple of days) and other old-fashioned-type books.

He had to go, but he taught me and my grubby socks the steps for a basic foxtrot dance in the kitchen before he left.

'How come you know all this again?'

'In school we have a choice between this, running laps of the grounds in the freezing cold or playing chess with the maths teacher.'

'Got it. It's not an all-boys school is it?'

And for this I got a well-deserved fake punch and a loud 'NO!'

And then I was on my own again, and quite

pleased about the dancing.

Then I chilled and read a bit, and tried to make my long black dress look like something a bit more stylish by taking up the hem, but that didn't work and now I will have to cut it even shorter and use it as a top. I should have measured it properly instead of just using the edge of a cracker box as a guideline. I didn't let on why I didn't show up at the tearoom until five. Didn't want to give Jackson the pleasure of seeing me make a fool of myself again. I borrowed Aunt Maisie's vintage white top to wear with my beaded jeans and it sort of suits me.

The others were all talking at me the same time, which made it sound like Chinese, and it took a bit of brain work to catch what they were on about. Anyway, THE NEWS: Bob's parents are organising a formal ball (aka party for posh people) in honour of his grandfather. No-one is saying it, but I think they're scared it might be the last time he'll be able to enjoy a ball and know what's going on.

Bob's dad left this morning after Bob and Jackson had shown him what we were doing with the tearoom. Jackson said that as soon as he saw it, he got quite emotional and said how there used to be balls and parties there all the time when he and

Jackson's mum were little. So they decided to hold the meal in the courtyard and then everyone would come across to the tearoom for the drinks and dancing part of the evening. There's only a short time to organise it so the whole family is pulling together with Bob and Jackson doing the stuff here and the adults doing the phone stuff. It will be all long dresses and tuxedos.

OK, the best bit is that ME AND JENNY ARE INVITED!!!! The second best bit is that the four of us are in charge of decorating the tearoom. I have not been this into something in *years*!! The third best bit is that it will not be anything like the party my mum and dad had four years ago when I had to wear a corduroy dress and hand out swirled cream-cheese on ritz crackers with chives sprinkled over. At least I hope not. Corduroy should be illegal.

We went down to the Gate Lodge so I could call Aunt Maisie and tell her not to expect me back for dinner. She gets that it's a cool thing about this party and said to just ask if there was anything she could do. I told her yes, she could NOT tell my parents, and make sure they don't visit on the night of the party. She laughed and said, 'Done deal, little one.'

Jenny, Bob, Jackson and I, then spent the whole

evening around the kitchen table in the Gate Lodge planning and eating quiches and salad, and these amazing apple puff pastry things, which were so good that I asked Nanny Gloria for the recipe.

Jenny and Bob loved all each other's ideas immediately, so me and Jackson had to fight pretty hard to keep things fair and realistic. Jackson is taking it pretty well the way Jenny is so besotted with Bob, and the way Bob seems to be equally into her. Maybe Jackson's not as crazy about her as I first thought.

Apparently even Mr Walsh is thrilled about the party, which is completely amazing, even spooky.

DAY 2

I now hate my clothes.

I know I say I hate everything, but I really *do* hate my clothes. They are more stylish than the clothes most girls I know wear, but compared to Jenny and Aunt Maisie I feel really dull and unimaginative. Black stuff doesn't seem to work outside the city.

I said this to Aunt Maisie just now at breakfast because she doesn't judge me. My mother would say, 'Well, at last you are seeing some sense', and I'd want to take back whatever I had just said. I probably will go back to liking that stuff again, it's just that people here don't dress like that.

***

LATER

Aunt Maisie came in while I was writing the stuff just above this, and we drove for an hour to get to the nearest big town. We bought me four outfits, which we can make eight or more outfits from by swapping the pieces around. There is a pink dress (NOT pastel pink), a blue dress, a white skirt, cream trousers, four different tops, two cardigans, a little jumper, and three pairs of shoes that are the size of my feet, unlike my usual boots, which are the size of a small family car. The new outfits look *really* fashionable and amazing, but I am a little bit afraid they will make my brain seize-up and make me all ordinary. No, they are too cool to make me ordinary, they might make people say things though, like Jackson might think that I did it because of what he said. Well, I'll just have to show him that it doesn't make any difference what I wear, I am still my own person and I do what I want.

We got *so* much stuff including earrings and bracelets and underwear. It cost a fortune and I felt bad about that but Aunt Maisie said it is my wedding present, just a few years early (more than 'a few', I hope! I have no plans to get married until I'm at least thirty). Next week we are going back to find a party dress, which I guess is to celebrate my university graduation! Aunt Maisie is SO COOL. I wish she was my mother.

I am completely excited! I have been trying them all on in different combinations and I look so different. Now the thing is that my hair looks like it's just hanging there because, well, it's just hanging there. Jenny is good at doing stuff with her hair so she's coming over now to help me with that. I'm going to wear one of the outfits later this afternoon (I think the white skirt and the white and pink sleeveless top) when we meet Jackson and Bob in the village to buy more paint.

***

LATER

Bob didn't notice the new look because he's only met me a couple of times, but Jackson was staring at me like I had a turnip for a head.

'Wow,' was what he eventually came out with, which was pretty cool. I mean not that I care what he thinks, it's just nice when anyone has a good reaction to you.

'Say anything, and you're dead,' I snarled.

Which wasn't the ladylike effect I'm going for, but if

he had laughed I would've had to have gone home and never left the house again.

'Can I say, "Wow", again?'

'No,' I said with my teeth gritted, but he made me laugh.

We bought some gold paint to add a bit of something to the tearoom chairs, and some more lavender and some white to finish the walls and woodwork.

Jackson paid, and the boys carried all the bags. Normally I would have insisted on carrying one to show I wasn't all weak and helpless, but somehow my new outfit made me not want to carry anything. I guess that's how princesses feel. When I am older I will employ someone to carry things so I won't have to – books, bags, plates, suitcases. Or just get married, which is pretty much the same.

We were headed out and saw this man on the street opposite, leaving a building, slamming the door behind him like he was a huffy kid.

'Isn't that the Park manager?' asked Bob.

It was Mr Walsh, coming out of a small, deserted-looking warehouse on the other side of the road. Jenny said it used to be the storage warehouse for an oil merchants, from before the farmers around started to get deliveries straight to their own farms from the suppliers.

'The estate owns some property in the village, but not that building,' Jackson said.

He looked at me like he knew I'd be up for it and said, 'Let's see what's inside.'

'Good idea,' I said and we headed out the door.

Bob and Jenny thought we were being silly (which coming from them is a bit rich!), and wanted to get back to the tearoom. So we went inside, while they kept watch. Jackson gave Pie to Jenny to make sure he wouldn't escape inside the warehouse.

The hinges were broken, so although the door was padlocked we could push our way in.

It was a small enough room for a warehouse, and there were a few large oil barrels and some building equipment, hammers and rope and a lever thing. I was hoping for a trap door or some stolen goods, but it was all quite boring really and we felt a bit nothing when we told the others what was in there.

Jackson saw my pissed-off look and whispered right into my ear, 'It could still be important Tia, we might be able to work out what he's up to.'

Once we got back to the tearoom there wasn't much of a chance for any of us to talk because we had so much grafting to get done. I didn't have to be careful not to get paint and dirt on my new clothes because Bob had brought along some of his old shirts for us to wear as overalls and they reached mine and Jenny's knees which made the guys start calling us 'the elves'. Once all the walls were done (two in lavender, two in white, with white on the window frames) we voted to leave the chairs for another day as it's such a big job. Instead we stripped the old paint from a long wooden sign where you could just about make out the words 'The New Park Tearoom'. Bob said that was the name they had given it in its last year of life, to try and attract some customers.

Jenny had the idea of renaming the tearoom. We all agreed to that, but wanted to take ideas from everyone because we were worried that with her in charge of the name it might end up being called 'Fluffy Singsong Tearoom' or something like that.

In fact Jenny suggested, 'The Cosy Tea Corner', which was quite reasonable, but a bit 'cottagey' for such a grand building.

Bob suggested something in Latin, just to show off that he knew Latin, and Jenny thought that was a better idea than hers.

Jackson suggested 'The Last Waltz Tearoom', which I thought was the best and I expected the others to vote for that. So I was *really* surprised when my suggestion of 'The Blue Lavender Tea Palace', led to a big 'YES!' from all of them. Naming tearooms, another thing I don't exactly suck at. The lettering will have to be done really well so Bob and Jenny have volunteered to work on a stencil for it in Nanny Gloria's house tomorrow morning. Bob is a bit of a showoff, but not badly enough that you wouldn't want to hang out with him. He's also way goofier even than Jackson, but he and Jenny are so sweet together. I hope he gets it together and kisses her soon.

Jackson pulled me aside and whispered in my ear (again, a lot of that going on with him lately!), asking me to meet him in the courtyard at ten o'clock tonight for more dancing.

I was so surprised or something that I forgot to answer, so he said, 'We only have two weeks until the party and I'll need you to dance with me so I don't have to waltz with all my great aunties and the women who do charity work with Bob's mother.'

'I'm sure they dance beautifully,' I said.

'They lead,' he said.

So I agreed to meet him at the courtyard at ten tonight, purely a charitable thing to benefit him, and because I have a goal to reach.

God this was a long day!! Usually I don't do this much in a week!

When I got back I had some oil on my new skirt (which must have come from the oil barrels in the warehouse) and was really upset, but luckily Aunt Maisie had a bottle of stuff that soon shifted it.

I told her that we had a meeting at the Big House and she said she wasn't happy about me being out that late, so I had to promise to be back by midnight. I put a cardigan over the white outfit. I'm now really confused because I love the new stuff but I don't feel that it's really me, and the old stuff isn't me either. So I can feel self-conscious but stylish and fun in the new stuff, or depressed and comfortable in the old stuff. I love the new clothes it's just that my personality hasn't grown into them yet.

When I was cycling over to the Park just before ten I remembered that they lock the gates at night, but this time Jackson was standing there with a key and he showed me that a spare was kept behind a nearby wooden post so now I can always get in. I thanked him and threatened to murder them all in their beds, which made him laugh. I left my bike leaning against the wall of the Gate Lodge we ran through the Park in the pitch darkness all the way to the courtyard. Now that I think of it, I don't know why we ran, it was just kind of exciting to be doing something in secret in the dark.

He got straight to it and taught me how to do a whole foxtrot. He had turned on the lights of the sitting room, which gave us enough light to see how badly I was doing. I kept stepping when I should be bouncing, and bouncing when I should be stepping, and going back on my left foot twice instead of backwards and then forwards. Then he produced a portable sound system from behind a pillar, which made me nervous about someone hearing us.

'Grandfather is the only one around and he's not likely to hear,' Jackson reminded me.

'And Bob?'

'Not here.'

'Where's he gone to? There's nowhere to go around here.'

'I meant sleeping, he sleeps like a log.'

But Jackson is a really bad liar, he went totally red. Bob must have been with Jenny.

It felt *fantastic* dancing to real music rather than

just music in my head. I stepped on Jackson's toes a lot, but these new shoes are a lot less clumpy, in fact they are rather dainty. The only problem is that I am not. Still, I'm getting better.

I caught sight of the time on Jackson's watch and it was ten to midnight. I said I had to run and he laughed and called me Cinderella and ran back with me to the gates. I grabbed my bike and cycled off and didn't catch what he said as I left.

DAY 23

I can't *believe* I thought I would be bored here. Something really amazing happened today. Well, it's not a good thing but it's a good thing for me, and it means that I get to help out that elderly couple from the village with the uneaten fruitcake. I got a call from Jenny and the old man had another fall and had to go back to hospital and so they needed someone to mind their insane dog Buddy.

Apparently Nanny Gloria is very strict about no animals because, as she said, 'she likes everything spick and span and her floors clean enough to eat off', (which doesn't make sense as Buddy is the only one of us who would actually eat off a floor, and therefore make her happy). But Aunt Maisie said I could keep Buddy here if I take full responsibility and make up a bed for him in the shed.

I have just spent the last hour tidying everything in the shed away neatly and making a space for his bed. I am now getting good at tidying and cleaning and it feels so good that I've no idea what my problem was with it before. It's like how I couldn't eat peas for years and then one day I suddenly couldn't get enough of them. Jenny called around with three old blankets and we put these in a big cardboard box that I cut the front off.

I hope Buddy gets on OK with all of us, especially Pie.

Then Jenny and I rode over to collect Buddy. On the way I teased her about meeting Bob last night, but she genuinely didn't know what I was talking about. She couldn't deny that she likes him, I mean, she redoes her nail polish every day now. She is still not sure if he likes her. Well, she is, but saying she isn't means that I say all the things she wants to hear.

We glimpsed Buddy through the window of the house and he looked so sad all on his own. I had forgotten how scruffy he is, and because he is a medium-sized dog he doesn't look cute, just scruffy and light brown. In fact he has to be the worst looking dog I have ever seen. I bet the other dogs play with him only out of pity. But he obviously doesn't know because he thinks he's the business, strutting around showing us his toys. He was a bit confused when we put all his stuff into a couple of plastic bags and tied them to our handlebars. I loosely fastened his leash to the back carrier and we cycled slowly back to Aunt Maisie's with him running behind, really loving it.

A hose-bath on the lawn was the first thing, because he was a bit stinky. I used this great apple-scented shampoo so he now smells like dessert. You're probably not supposed to use human shampoo on a dog, but who cares.

We left Buddy in Aunt Maisie's shed and went to the tearoom, that is, the Tea Palace (God it's going to take me forever to remember that, and I was the one who came up with the name!). We sort of got some things done, but Jenny and I wanted to get back to Buddy, and Jackson and Bob were yawning their heads off and not paying us any attention. So we agreed to meet back tomorrow afternoon. The afternoons are best because the coach tours of the Big House are usually from ten to twelve in the morning and one of them has to be there as the guide. Jackson and Bob say it's fine to bring Buddy tomorrow as long as he doesn't knock things over with his tail and can make friends with Pie.

***

LATER

I got a flashlight and a cushion and went and read with Buddy in his shed. Well, I was reading *Jane Eyre* (which I have been missing) and he was just looking at me waiting for me to do something interesting. It was not the best place to be reading it because it has all got a bit mental with this mad servant and ghostly laughs and someone setting fire to Mr Rochester's room. Every time Buddy moved, I jumped about a mile.

I would have been out there half the night, only my brother Aidan phoned. We talked for about thirty minutes and he sounded really excited about his summer courses and he said that I sounded really great too. I was a bit sad when I got off the phone and felt like I wanted to kick something. So Aunt Maisie made us some scones and a hot malt drink, and I felt much better. I went out and gave Buddy one last hug before bedtime and explained why he had to sleep outside and he licked my face as if to tell me everything was fine. He is braver than me. You have to be very brave to be happy I think.

DAY 24

I had to cycle to the village for more dog food and I noticed that someone had fixed the door on the old warehouse. There was no time to investigate because I had a hungry dog waiting back at Aunt Maisie's.

My plan was to fill Buddy up so completely that he wouldn't want to go snacking on Pie. Unfortunately this meant he couldn't run as fast as usual and it took us forever to get to the Tea Palace (there, look at that, right name first time!).

I held Buddy's collar while he sniffed at Pie, who was being held by Jackson. They stayed sniffing at each other for a minute before Buddy gave Pie a lick and then barked at me as if to say he approved. As the day wore on, Buddy got so protective of Pie that the only one who can now get near the little bunny is Jackson, Buddy keeps the rest of us away from his new little pal.

I could hear Jenny teasing Bob about his yawning. Jackson and I were prepping the chairs, and when he let out a huge yawn for the millionth time in five minutes, I said to him, 'Come on, what's going on at night? And you are a terrible liar so don't even try it.'

He glanced at Bob before coming clean.

'OK, we might as well tell you. The other night on the way back from the Gate Lodge really late, we thought we saw someone running towards the Tea Palace.'

'We ran after them,' Bob continued, 'But they were much faster than us. Which is how we know it wasn't Mr Walsh. So for the past two nights we've been taking it in turns to wait up and see if someone shows.'

Bob admitted that he fell asleep on his watch the first night, but that last night he did see someone at about one-thirty in the morning. He watched where the man went but he seemed to disappear around where the stone hut is.

They looked completely wrecked so Jenny and I

offered to meet them tonight, that way we can all hide in different parts of the Park and have more chance of catching him.

It was time for a flapjack break, sitting on the cushions and things, and the guys fell asleep. We sneaked off and left a note in Jackson's non-Pie pocket to tell them we'd meet them at midnight by the gates. I can't wait!

When I was cycling out of the Park with Buddy in tow, Mr Walsh was coming in. We said hello and he smiled and nodded back, so maybe he's not so bad and we're just making stuff up about him. What if that's true, what if he's just ordinary, like my dad, and we are such an ulcer that he's stressed and mean whenever he sees us. He had white paint on his hands, so he must have started work on the east wing. That 'win" stuff is so funny, it makes it sound like they live in an aeroplane.

Aunt Maisie said I could stay over at Jenny's tonight as long as she spoke to Nanny Gloria and cleared it with her first. I have collected black boots and trousers for me and Jenny to wear as night-camouflage and black sweaters and t-shirts for all of us. There you go, at least it's good for something! I'm off now. I think it will be fun, much better than hanging around town late at night staring at groups of guys and girls we hardly know. I wonder how Dee and Kira are doing. I wonder if Mum and Dad have done anything unforgivable to my bedroom.

DAY 25

Last night at Jenny's we did the real cliché thing of pretending we were tired early and going upstairs. We changed into the black clothes and got into bed and put the lights out. Jenny said that Nanny Gloria's snoring is enough to register on some earthquake instruments two countries over. It was SO obvious as soon as she was sleeping.

We couldn't stop giggling all the way downstairs. Buddy couldn't believe his luck when we came outside to the rug where we had tied him by his leash to wait for us.

Jackson and Bob were waiting by the gates and put the black sweaters on over their t-shirts.

'Tia is in charge of the world's supply of black

clothes,' Jackson explained to Bob, who nodded as if it were actually true.

As he outlined the plan, Jackson became so soldier-like and military that Jenny got another giggling fit and had to pretend to fix Buddy's collar while she recovered.

The plan was that Jenny and Bob would take one side of the Park and Jackson and I would take the other. I asked Bob how much he paid Jackson to put that in the plan, and he grinned and said, 'Jackson didn't put up much of a fight on that one,' and then for some reason he winked at me.

'Make sure to concentrate on what we are doing here, catching that man,' Jackson warned them as they ran off toward the Blue Lavender Tea Palace.

Which left me, Jackson, Buddy and Pie.

By the time we were sitting on the ground behind a large tree near the hut, I simply had to know. It was as if the fact that it was so dark that I couldn't see his face, made me brave enough to ask.

'I thought maybe you might want to be with Jenny?'

Although I couldn't see his reaction it was like I could feel it.

'God, No! I mean, not in the way I think you're implying.'

He was genuinely surprised, and I was completely confused (and not just because he used the word 'implying' when fifty easier ones could have done the job).

'But when I first met you, you were always talking to her and looking at her...'

'I'm just not good around new people so I tend to focus on whoever I'm already comfortable with, and I've known Jenny ever since I can remember. She's like a sister to me. I know people say that a lot, but it's true, especially as I don't have any sisters, just a brother.'

Then he pretended that he heard someone coming, just so he didn't have to talk any more.

We sat in the dark in total silence for about an hour. It was funny, but I felt really calm, just listening to me and Jackson and Buddy breathing. Sometimes we'd breathe at the same time for a while and then at different times. At one point I thought he was touching my hand, but it was Pie who had clambered out of his pocket and was pushing against my little finger with his nose. At that point I got worried in case Buddy was doing something similar and Jackson was thinking that it was me trying to get close. I know that's a mental thing to think, but it worried me so much that I said,

'Let's go, there's no-one coming.'

He said, 'I thought you were adventurous.'

And I said that I *am* adventurous, and that real adventures are not about developing haemorrhoids from sitting on wet grass all night.

'There's only one thing to do with you when you get like this Tia.'

'What?' I said, in my most 'back-off' voice.

Then he jumped up, pulled me to my feet and started to dance with me in tiny steps, holding me really close and very quietly singing the tune in my ear. I started to giggle immediately, and he said, 'See ... not so tough.'

At that exact moment Buddy started to growl softly, but he is not territorial about me the way he is about Pie, so I knew there must be someone coming.

It turned out to be a deer. There's a small herd of them living in the fields on the opposite side of the lake to the Big House and the Blue Lavender Tea Palace. I was getting really tired and so was Jackson, and we had the bright idea that we could take a nap and Buddy could wake us when he sensed someone near. Just as I was about to close my eyes I caught sight of some stars between the branches.

In the end it was Bob and Jenny who woke us up, not Buddy. Jenny was laughing at us both being asleep, but Bob got really angry, which is a bit much seeing as how he fell asleep the other night and didn't have a dog to sound the alarm.

Jackson explained that we had only fallen asleep half-an-hour before and that Buddy would have growled and woken us if anyone had come along. But Bob just wouldn't let it go and kept on complaining until I finally lost it.

'Bob, if you're so into catching this person, how come you're back over here and not in the Tea Palace keeping a watch out there? And don't you think all your shouting has scared anyone away?'

'Well if it hasn't, yours certainly has,' he yelled back at me.

Jenny looked like she was going to cry and Jackson was completely fed up. I just grabbed Jenny and Buddy and went back to the Gate Lodge without even saying goodbye to Jackson.

Jenny wanted me to go back and make up, but I don't see why I should have to, after all, Bob was mean to me first. Because I was in such a mood I didn't really talk to her either and then she got worried that I was angry at her.

I think it is because her parents are diplomats and probably don't yell much that she can't handle it when people fall out. With me, I just feel so bad that I have to lose my temper so that the situation goes away, or I get to go away or something.

Not that I feel good about it, it's just what I do. Today I'm really pissed off with myself for reacting that way. I could have just seen it as Bob being in a mood and let him get on with it. But OH NO, I just have to wade in there shouting and sulking every time. From now on I must be nice no matter what I think. Great dancers are always very mannerly and lovely.

As I left the Gate Lodge around noon today I told Jenny not to worry, it would all be fine. We agreed to give the Tea Palace a rest for today and just do stuff on our own.

I just got a phone call from Jackson who has called a peace meeting tomorrow so we can work things out. I feel like wearing my jeans and long black sweater and my oldest boots, like I will be safer in that outfit.

Buddy made me feel better, licking my face and putting his head on my knee as I sat reading in the garden.

Tonight I got a call from Kira. It was really strange because although I loved talking to her and we stayed on the phone for over an hour, I feel like my life here is my real life and what goes on back there is someone else's life. When she was talking about what they did in town and at Dee's oldest brother's party, it didn't sound nearly as good as it would have before.

Then I went back into the living room but couldn't concentrate on *Jane Eyre* so I chatted with Aunt Maisie and told her more about Jenny and Bob and how Jackson doesn't like her after all, and about what a pain Jackson is because he is always so in charge of what we are doing, even though he is the best at it. It would just be nice if he let someone else be in charge.

'Like you?' she asked.

'Exactly.'

'By the way Tia, how many Jacksons are there?' Aunt Maisie asked.

I didn't know what she meant.

'Well you tell me about how he helped you with your dancing and then you say he is really selfish, and then that he is really stupid but then there's a really funny story he told. I've counted about twenty

Jacksons, some terrible and some wonderful, so which is the real Jackson?'

Just then something totally ridiculous happened, I burst out crying because I suddenly realised that I'm really horrible about people all the time. I think it's so they don't attack me, or if I tell myself that they are useless then I don't have to worry that they might not like me.

Aunt Maisie got all concerned and put down her crossword. 'Oh Tia, sweetheart, I was only joking. What's the matter?'

I blurted out how I hate the way that I find all the bad things all the time and that I want to be more like Jenny because she sees the good things and doesn't lose her temper. Once I started I was on a sort of roll and couldn't stop the words coming out. That's how I ended up telling her about Trundle and how much I hated my life back home and how everyone thought I was trouble, but I'm not but now I don't know how to get out of it because everyone expects me to not do work and be all sulky. I just went on and on for ages and ages, and at some stage I stopped crying and just kept talking. She is so cool, she didn't try and help or anything she just listened.

'So there you have it!' I sort of grinned when I ran

out of things to say.

Aunt Maisie said that she was really glad that I had shared it all with her and promised we would get it all sorted without telling Mum and Dad more than was good for their blood pressure. She made me feel a bit better about Mum anyway. She said she thinks that Mum just isn't really into hugging and stuff, probably because she didn't get much attention or many hugs herself when she was little – she was the oldest and she always had to help around the house a lot and didn't get much time to do her own thing. Now that I think about it, she doesn't hug anyone, not even Dad, so it's not like it's personal. And maybe she doesn't ask me to do much work around the house because *she* always had to when she was young and wants me to have more free time ... I never thought of it that way, I always just got pissed off at the mess. I feel a bit bad now that she does so much good stuff for people and I just moan because she's not doing things for me. When I get back maybe I'll join in with the kids' clubs more, or help her run the fund raisers or something.

Maybe Jackson feels bad about things too and I just don't notice because I am so busy feeling shit about my own stuff. I always think that everyone else has a great life and is doing better than me, but maybe that's not their take on it at all.

CRYING
ING
CRYING.
CRYING.
CRYING
G
CRYING

DAY 26

As soon as I woke up I went around to Jenny's and she looked as if she had been crying *way* more than me. The red eyes and puffy face were a dead giveaway even though she planted a big grin on her as if everything was fine. I'm so used to having arguments with people that it doesn't affect me so much, but she was really upset. I felt really bad about that. I gave her a big hug and we both felt way better.

She explained that it wasn't so much the argument between me and Bob that got to her, it was that it made her think about how her mum wasn't there for her to discuss it with. Her parents only come to see her twice a year and then she flies to them over the Christmas holidays.

'If I could have any wish in the world,' she said, 'It would be that my mum and dad would make more of an effort to spend time with me in the summer.'

I asked why she doesn't go to them and she explained that they are in a country where there are no English or French speaking people around, and that because they are always on duty they are always having to go off and do things and she just gets left on her own, sometimes not even seeing them for days.

I now feel that I have been really exaggerating my situation at home. Although Mum and Dad don't get in most days until late, at least they talk to me and we eat together on the weekends. Also I've had Aidan to talk to, poor Jenny is an only child.

It's like what I was thinking the other night, that I think that I am the only one with problems and that everyone else is fine. I never would have guessed that Jenny could possibly feel bad about her life.

We did our hair in really cool styles and went down to the Blue Lavender Tea Palace for the meeting. I was wearing my new stuff, but also these striped tights that make the outfit look more young and rockstar than older film star, if you know what I mean. I also wore one of the bracelets around my ankle and threaded a necklace through my hair. It sounds all weird, but it really looked amazing.

The atmosphere was a bit funny at first and everyone was pretending to be doing things with cloths or paint brushes so we wouldn't have to look at each other.

Just as Jackson called us to one of the tables to talk, Buddy lay down at Jackson's feet and Pie climbed up on his back and stayed there. It was so cute, just like one of the greetings cards where the dog, the cat and the mouse all get along and sit by the fire. We were all laughing at this so it wasn't too hideous when Jackson set down some rules about us speaking nicely to each other and getting along while we decorate the Blue Lavender Tea Palace. We also decided that whatever Mr Walsh might be up to it wasn't worth our being tired and snapping at each other, so we're going to leave all that well alone, at least until after the party.

I took a deep breath and said, 'Bob I'm really sorry for getting so angry with you the other night. I realise that you were frustrated when we feel asleep. I felt angry because I didn't think you needed to keep going on about it. And I shouldn't have shouted and

I'm sorry.'

I was all shaky by the time I said it, and Jenny put her hand on mine to make me feel calmer. (I had written the words on a piece of paper at Jenny's and practised it a few times, guess those therapy sessions did teach me something after all!!)

Bob gave me a hug and muttered, 'I'm sorry too', and that was the end of it. Big relief.

While we were painting the chairs (which is a MUCH bigger job than we thought) Bob asked Jackson if Mr Walsh would have the east wing (wing! – still hilarious) finished in time for the party, Jackson said that Mr Walsh would want to get started on it soon if that was the plan.

But when we saw Mr Walsh a couple of days ago at the gate, he had white paint on his hands. I immediately wanted to talk about what the paint was doing on his hands when they hadn't started painting yet, but as we'd all just promised not to focus on it, I had to change the subject. When Jenny and Bob ran to the Big House for bottles of water, Jackson showed me some more dance moves and we practised the waltz and the foxtrot. I am now getting the steps right but I don't look like a dancer yet. The rest of the afternoon was just chairs and more chairs. Tonight I will dream about chairs, I just know it.

This evening the old lady phoned to thank me for looking after Buddy. Her husband had his hip operation and is feeling much better, but they won't be home for at least another couple of weeks. I told her to relax about Buddy, and that he is running through the lavender field for most of every day and has made friends with a grey baby rabbit. This made her laugh and she sounded relieved. It feels really good to be able to help someone like this, someone I don't even know. When I get back home I'm going to find out if there are any people who need help with walking their dogs or looking in on their cats while they are away in hospital or wherever. It makes me sort of get why Mum and Dad do all their volunteer stuff, it makes you feel like you are making a difference in the world.

I know I promised to give it a rest, but still can't stop wondering why Mr Walsh had the paint on his hands and what's going on with the warehouse in the village and the man in the Park at night. I decided I'm going to get to the Park really early tomorrow morning, before Jackson and Bob are up, and have a look around by myself. This time I'll have

Buddy to warn me if anyone is around.

I noticed that I now stand and walk like Jenny, really straight with my shoulders back. I don't know if that's from being around her or from the dancing. I'm going to have a bath with rose petals and that fancy bubble-bath now, as I haven't done that in a while.

PINK DRESS

DAY 27

I woke up early and put on the pink dress. I also wore this little diamond thing in my hair, which Jenny lent me the last time, and a pink and silver bracelet which we got with the dress. Last night after my bath I was up in the attic with Aunt Maisie and she showed me some boxes of clothes from years ago. Some of them are amazing and they mix with my old and new clothes in really great ways. So now I am a million percent comfortable with how I look, princess and old fashioned dancer and rock star all at the same time.

When I get home I want to throw out all the old ugly stuff in my room and start gradually collecting beautiful things like old leather books and the other stuff Aunt Maisie has. I noticed that the lavender that Jackson first left on the doorstep is now completely past it, but I haven't the heart to just throw it out.

Buddy and I got to the Park just as the sun came up and I opened the gate with the spare key. The rays looked so incredible through the leaves of the trees, and glinting on the water. First I looked inside the little hut as I remembered we hadn't actually opened the door of it that night, and thought maybe a homeless man might be sleeping there. But it was empty except for Pie's old box which was now on the bench instead of the floor.

Next we went up to the Big House which was a bit scary until I reminded myself that Jackson's grandfather can't hear well and doesn't wake until ten, and that Bob and Jackson both sleep until about nine.

I peered through all of the downstairs windows and saw nothing. I guess I just wanted a mystery so much that my head made one up out of ordinary things. I didn't feel bad though, because I was sitting on the steps up to the courtyard and imaging what it will look like when the party is on.

NOTE TO SELF: Get dress for party soon or I

might end up with something orange or something that makes me look scrawny, or illegal, or wrong for other reasons.

I didn't really notice that Buddy had started jumping about as I was so lost in daydreaming. Jackson appeared and I tried to look like I was part of the brickwork. Nonchalant does work well when you need it.

He looked like he didn't know what to say either, and I didn't want to let on that I was still investigating, so I said, 'I thought you might be up and about, so I kindly came over to give you the privilege of being able to dance with me.'

Then I thought that might make it look like I fancy him so I kept babbling.

'Yes, I imagined all those mothers and old aunts wanting to haul you around the dance floor and thought I would do you a favour by coming around here so you could teach me how to dance so I can save you at the party,' I said.

'You're going to save me?' He was laughing by now but I couldn't back out.

'So let's get on with it then,' I said, as if mildly annoyed at having to be there for him.

'Absolutely. And thank you Tia, this is very

thoughtful of you.'

God, I could die when I think of it now!

We spent the next age dancing in the courtyard, doing a waltz, a foxtrot, a quickstep (my favourite!) and a Viennese waltz, which makes you feel a bit sick from all the spinning. He also taught me the basic steps for the rumba. There is so much to learn but I'm loving it.

Just as I was doing a really strange rumba move, Bob arrived, and I said hello and said I had to leave and walked away.

This time Jackson followed me and asked me to sit down and help him plan the lights for the Tea Palace. So we sat on the grass by the lake and talked.

We then went on to talk about ourselves and I told him about my brother Aidan and my parents. This time I said the good things about them rather than moaning. I said about all the people they help and how patient they are when I get into trouble. I didn't mention the trouble much because I feel like that was the old me and now I'd never do half the things I used to, or even three-quarters of them. Or actually I don't know if I'd be bothered with any of it now. Maybe just talking back when people are being ridiculous.

I asked him didn't he mind going to boarding school, and he said he loves it. The reason he and his brother go there is because their mum and dad work late during the week. I also found out that he gets home every weekend and that his favourite thing is to go down to the river behind the house and watch this pair of otters who have lived there for years and have brought up loads of cubs. He also fishes and helps the local farmers with fencing and herding sheep.

It's funny but although I like Jackson here, I know that if I was back in town with Dee and Kira and all the people we know, I'd be the first to laugh at Jackson and make fun of the way he dresses and talks because it's so different from us. That really sucks because I must have seemed really different to him and he still made me feel really welcome and taught me to dance and everything. I guess that makes him a better person than me. I feel like everyone is a better person than me.

We talked until it was nearly lunchtime so I came back here to eat. Now I have to rush over to the Tea Palace so I'm not late meeting the others.

***

LATER

RESULTS OF BIG PLANNING MEETING: We decided to put little twinkle lights in the trees outside, to make blue-lavender-coloured shades for the ceiling lights (with new bulbs) to give a colourful glow, to put little rose trees in earthenware pots around the room and add more twinkle lights to these. We also want to have sprigs of lavender at each table that people can take home with them.

Mr Walsh came in while we were there and was amazingly un-psycho as he said, 'Hello kids, just so you know there will be lots of extra vans, lorries and people around, because we are starting to paint the east wing and because we have some of the catering equipment arriving early for the party. Just so you know.'

I have to go now because Aunt Maisie has made me some hot chocolate.

DAY28

I was a bit surprised and shocked and amazed to get an early phone call from Bob. (You know the way there are people who phone you and people who don't?) He said the workmen had arrived to start to prepare to paint the east wing (still funny!) and Jackson had gone for the morning to find small rose trees in a plant nursery and Jenny was washing a car for a busy mother from the village. So he asked me would I come over to the Big House to help. I didn't ask 'with what?' because I wanted to sound helpful. I brought my book in case he kept me hanging around.

When I met Bob he showed me the guest list for the party and there were loads of lords and ladies and earls of places. It was fun until I noticed that some of them had a 'T' beside their name, including me and Jenny and about twenty others. Bob explained that it was for 'teenager' so we could all sit at tables beside each other. I guess I presumed that it would just be the four of us and a bunch of adults, but now there will be loads of others that Bob and Jackson know better, and we probably won't get to talk to the guys all night. There are at least ten girls coming and I bet they all dance brilliantly and Jackson has been teaching me just so I don't come over as a total embarrassment in front of his friends. It was a bit of a downer, but at least I'm still invited to the best party I'll ever get to go to. Maybe one of the teenage guys who's coming will dance with me and maybe he will be really polite about it when I mess up and say I was 'awfully interesting' at dancing.

Bob showed me into the large formal drawing room which looked onto the start of the east wing. He wanted me to hang out there for 'security reasons', which I took to mean I was to make sure no-one nicked the paintings. He had to look after something for his grandfather's nurse and as he ran off he said that the tours have been cancelled until after the party so no-one should bother me.

I was wearing my new blue dress, and a great vintage grey jacket, with my old grey shredded cardigan underneath and the whole thing looked 'rebellious rich kid' and matched the amazing furniture perfectly. I couldn't believe I was in such an incredible place, and doing them a favour by being there! Every inch of the room was beautiful, the gold line that went all the way around the wall, the painting of ladies and angels and sky on the ceiling, the lion paws on the ends of the chair legs, everything. I sat there reading *Jane Eyre* sometimes, and looking around sometimes.

Buddy sat on the rug (which was the size of a carpet in most peoples' houses) in front of the fireplace. It was as if he knew to be really well behaved as he just lay there staring at me the way he does when he's guarding Pie.

Every time though! Jackson does it every time! One minute I was on my own on the chair and the next moment he was crouching right beside me.

'Good book?' he said.

'Very,' I said, pretending I had known he was there.

It's funny how I don't feel I have to be all smart with him any more. He said the workmen had stopped for lunch and so should we. He'd brought a pizza and it felt so funny sitting there in such a luxurious and enormous room eating a cheese and mushroom pizza straight from the box. Bob smelled the pizza from upstairs and joined us, and I don't know why, but that seemed to make it not so good, although there was plenty of pizza. I must make more of an effort to get to know Bob, if only for Jenny's sake.

The Blue Lavender Tea Palace looks completely different from when we first started. The sign is up and the walls and woodwork are all done and it's starting to feel magical.

Jenny was hilarious she was so giddy, and Bob kept staring at her when he thought no-one else was looking. Somewhere between the first round of raspberry-bran-crunchies (which I made last night) and the end of the afternoon, we lost Buddy. He was gone for an hour, and images of me having to go to the hospital and tell the old couple and them dying from the shock of it, raced through my mind. I could hear him somewhere off in the Park, barking in the distance, but none of us could find him. Jackson offered to cycle around the Park and the village to find him, but I said I was sure he'd come back once he got hungry. Sure enough, as we were re-doing that stretch of window frame which we'd messed up before, Buddy reappeared. He had a small bit of white paint on him (not the same shade as our white) so he must have been in the east wing. It's funny how you can very easily become an expert in shades of white paint. Luckily Mr Walsh didn't show up to shout at us. We'll have to keep the doors closed from now on.

Anyway, we finished the window frame and the chairs (finally!) and after I got back I read *Jane Eyre* because I'm so into it after this morning. The story is *so* sad. Jane is away from Mr Rochester and really misses him and thinks she hears him calling her. She had rushed back to him and I stopped reading at that point just in case he isn't there and she has to be lonely for the rest of her life. I don't think I could recover from that, at least not tonight, so I'll finish it tomorrow.

DAY 29

Breakfast, Tea Palace, arranging stuff, hanging things, no dancing, no real conversations as everyone was so busy.

It's now ten at night and I have just finished reading *Jane Eyre* and I want to start it all over again. Jane is amaaaaazing. She went back to the house she used to work in as a governess and it's all destroyed from the fire. So she goes to a house nearby and that's where Mr Rochester is, and he can't believe she's come back because he was despairing. She doesn't care that his face is all burnt and he's blind and missing a hand (seriously!), she just loves him. I couldn't stop crying at that bit, I've turned into such a sap. The most amazing thing is that she doesn't care what he looks like, she just feels better when she's around him, and it doesn't matter what anybody else in the world might think about him looking like a bad imitation of a burger and her being nothing (although she is now rich because of someone leaving her a fortune). It's made me think about how I feel really good with Jenny and Jackson and Bob and really bad with the people in town and at the parties back home. I finally get it, that it's about how you feel and not what people say about who is or isn't cool or clever or whatever.

I am shallow, I'm so crap.

***

I was looking at the lavender in my bedroom today and was then wondering what outfit I should wear that Jackson hadn't seen, and I suddenly realised that I have a thing for him. That's my little secret, but I have a feeling Aunt Maisie guessed it before I did.

Maybe it's just because he is the only non-taken guy around, but maybe it's real. Anyway it doesn't matter because he probably sees me of more of a project than a person. Anyway if I can look amazing and dance really well at the party, then it will all have been worth it and I can feel like I was Rose Red or something at least for one night. I hope someone dances with me. I am going in to practise my hold in front of the bathroom mirror.

DAY 30

OK. WEIRDNESS!!! That idea about me learning to not care about how cool people are has all been a bit ruined. Jackson and Bob had been shopping for the lights for decorating in the morning, and we met them as usual just after lunch. They had obviously (I mean OBVIOUSLY) been clothes shopping too because Jackson was wearing a different kind of outfit than usual. It's radical, the kind of different that you don't dip into, like me and my recent change. It was still jeans, sneakers and t-shirt, but this new stuff didn't look like he'd borrowed it from his dad or whatever, it looked really good, like from a runway show or something. They'd also both had their hair cut different and they looked amazing.

'Say nothing,' Jenny whispered. 'Guys don't like you noticing that kind of thing.'

'How do you know?' I whispered back.

'They don't like people to think they care about how they look. I read it in a magazine. Ours is an all-girls' school, we read articles about boys all the time.' So we pretended nothing was different and the guys continued to look very pleased with themselves and Jackson didn't do much work.

Now I'm all pissed off because the girls at the party will all go for him now, and also now I don't get to be a better person. I can't go out with him now that he looks great because that would mean that I don't get to be mature about it, I might as well still be as shallow as a puddle in a heatwave. Anyway I don't know what I'm saying I just know that he has gone and ruined everything by getting a great haircut. Now he doesn't get to know that I liked him for being kind and patient and great to talk to. And won't get to be with him at all if there's that many girls coming to the party.

**

LATER

I had arranged to meet Jackson at eight for more

dancing, and now I take five times longer to get ready.

At first it was really fun, although now that I know I fancy him I'm *way* more self-conscious. We danced for almost two hours and he is teaching me new steps that build onto the basic ones so it all looks much fancier now. Plus, I'm not having to think and count all the time so it feels even better. Then as he was walking me back to my bike he started to talk about all the people that were coming to the party and about someone called Libby who I 'simply *have* to meet', and I got really jealous and starting thinking that everyone would have a good time and I'd be left sitting there like a lemon. I got really quiet and stopped answering him.

He copped on eventually and said, 'What is it? Did I say something wrong?'

'Forget it', I murmured.

'No.'

'What?'

'No, Tia, I won't forget it,' Jackson said. 'What's wrong? If you don't tell me then I can't help you and that's not fair on me or you.'

'Yeah, like you want to help me.'

'Of course I do, why wouldn't I? Do you think that I want you to feel bad?'

As soon as he said that I realised that was exactly what I thought, that people didn't care if I felt bad. I started to cry and turned away so he wouldn't see me.

'AND,' he said with a loud voice, but not shouting, 'You CAN be upset in front of people, in front of me at least, you don't have to get angry and storm off.'

I kept trying to hide my face from him, but he playfully pulled my hands away so I had to look him in the eye. As soon as I stopped fighting him he pulled me close in a huge hug.

He took me to the hut where we could sit down, and we talked about my parents and just, I don't know, stuff, and he had some cool things to say. We stayed there for about twenty minutes until we heard a rat scratching under the wooden floorboards of the hut. I ran out and he followed me, laughing and shaking his head saying 'Not so tough.' Then I was really tired and just wanted to get home.

I think I'm glad this happened, I'm not sure. The only down side is that if he ever did have any romantic ideas about me they are well and truly out the window. Still it's better that I know now rather than ending up getting all upset at the party.

DAY 31

Jenny and I found the perfect dresses today. Hers is red with a bow at the side and makes her look a bit older, and mine is midnight blue, which brings out my eyes, and has little diamondy beads and is cut low in the back. I kept staring and staring at myself in the mirror, I look that incredible in it. Tonight I am practising dancing in my new shoes until bedtime so I don't look like a wounded giraffe at the party.

DAY 32

I saw something when I went to the chemist in the village today. The man that I'd seen having the argument with Mr Walsh outside Aunt Maisie's house ages ago, he was coming out of the old warehouse building. He had a huge sack across his back filled with really heavy things.

I really want to work out what's happening, even if it's something as simple as them mending a pipe or something.

What I know so far:

- *Mr Walsh and this man have something to do with each other.*
- *Mr Walsh bought too much paint and started painting*

somewhere before the east wing was started.

- *I saw Mr Walsh on his hands and knees at the door of the hut the day we got the cushions and things from Jackson's room.*
- *Mr Walsh was upset about us using the Tea Palace.*
- *A man was running through the Park at night.*
- *They keep equipment in the warehouse.*

On a cop show they would have worked it out many ad breaks ago.

So my mind keeps skipping from being confused by that mystery and being freaked about the party.

Only three days to go! There are loads of caterers and people around the Park now so Jenny and I have decided to stay away until the actual night.

DAY 33

I just can't *believe* it. I can't understand. I am sitting here and waiting to wake up, but I'm not waking up so this is really happening to me. Aunt Maisie came in as usual this morning with a cup of tea, and this time she said, 'No matter what happens, everything is for the best,' just as she left the room. I soon found out what she was talking about because the moment I got downstairs Dad was there waiting for me and he looked *really* uncomfortable.

Dad said that Mum had sent him to pick me up. Apparently Mum was worried that I was too much trouble for Aunt Maisie and had booked me in to do a dressmaking course that the daughter of a friend of hers is going on.

Aunt Maisie told me that she *loved* having me here, and had been saying as much to Mum only two days ago. She tried to call Mum as I stood there in shock, but she was at work and wasn't answering. Dad just kept saying, 'I've been told to bring you home this morning,' so he was no use.

'Listen,' Aunt Maisie said, 'just go back for today and then I'll chat with them tonight and you'll be back here by the morning. I'll drive and fetch you myself.'

'But what about Buddy?'

'I'll take care of Buddy, it's just for today.'

So that's how I find myself right now back in my messy old bedroom, writing this. I feel like the world has ENDED. No Tea Palace, no Jenny and Bob, no Jackson, no fields of lavender, no Buddy, no Pie, no deer, no Park, no Aunt Maisie, no great food, no dancing, no party, no stars at night or anything. It's like none of the other stuff happened, that I just dreamed it. Now it's just the food-less kitchen, the living room and this messy bedroom. I could call Kira and Dee, but that would only make me feel worse. This is the first time I can remember when I have no interest in going into town. Before I left Aunt Maisie's I saw the bits of dried-up lavender in the pink glass bowl. I shoved them in my pocket. I keep feeling them there, and smelling them, to tell myself it was real. On the way back in the car I daydreamed about dancing with Jackson and now I might *never* get to do that again. Aunt Maisie says Mum will let me come back for the party at least, but she doesn't know her like I do.

***

LATER

Jenny just phoned and said to tidy my room! That made me laugh a bit, but then we were both crying. Aunt Maisie called too, and said not to worry she'd get it sorted. So I actually spent the last four hours cleaning up this room. It now is not-messy and the next task is to make it actually look interesting. I feel like I was on a great holiday and now I've been shoved into hell. I just can't stop thinking about how cruel it is. My stomach hurts.

MISTA

DAY 34

Last night Mum came home late and I made the mistake of immediately starting to tell her about the party and what an amazing time I was having there and how Aunt Maisie really wanted me there. Mum just said, 'You're staying here and going on the dressmaking course, I really went to a lot of trouble to get you on it at such short notice. Really Tia, you said a few weeks ago that you wanted to be a fashion designer. I feel that nothing I do ever makes you happy – you were begging me not to send you to your Aunt Maisie's and now if I send you back you'll just change your mind again!'

I could see her point, but my head got all muddled and I couldn't get the ideas sorted, so I just said thanks for getting me into the dressmaking course.

I couldn't sleep so I waltzed and foxtrotted my way around the room in the dark in the newly-cleared space, over and over as if I could dance it all away. I'm too tired of everything to be angry, I just feel really sad and I don't want to do anything.

I don't know what to do with myself tonight, especially as I've gone off television. Tomorrow is the day of the party and it looks like I'm not going to be there. I asked Jenny to take some pictures so at least I can see what it looked like. Aunt Maisie called and was very upset because she hasn't been able get hold of Mum on the phone to convince her to let me come back. She said she's going to look after Buddy until the old man comes out of hospital.

I have just spent the whole afternoon lying on my bed and staring at the ceiling. I was wondering what the guys will be wearing for the party, imagining Jenny and Bob dancing together, and remembering loads of stupid things from the last few weeks like the way Pie would stick his nose out from Jackson's pocket, the way Jenny laughs and moves her hands about as she talks, Nanny Gloria telling us to finish everything on our plates as if we were still three years old, the way Bob would always scratch his arm when thinking, the way Aunt Maisie would always give me a hug when I'd arrive back from being out somewhere. Mostly I was imagining the way Jackson's face wouldn't change if I made a mistake in dancing, the way he would just explain what to do and then smile when I got it right, even if it was something easy.

I wonder if they will ever find out why those weird things were happening with Mr Walsh?

***

LATER

What an *insane* life I am having! I am now back in my room at Aunt Maisie's house. I didn't run away or anything (although I did think about it). I couldn't have planned it better or stranger. Earlier tonight, Mum and Dad were sitting in the living room watching a political show and shaking their heads, and I was sitting there waiting for the best moment to talk with them. Then the doorbell went and I was cursing it because I thought it meant that Mum and Dad would have a visitor and be talking with them for hours and I wouldn't have a last chance to get to make Mum see sense.

Then it was like being on another planet because

Jackson and this well-dressed middle-aged woman walked in. I could tell it was his mother because she looked exactly like him, well except that she was a woman and pretty.

Then there was the awkward bit when no-one knows what to say, when my mother usually says, 'now then', and, 'good'. So, to cut a long story short, Jackson's mum wanted to talk to my mum and dad alone, so Mum asked me to bring Jackson with me into the kitchen.

We didn't want to miss anything, so we sat on the stairs in the hallway instead, on the second step. We couldn't hear the words, but we could hear how serious the voices were and that it was my mum doing most of the talking. Jackson took my hand as we sat there and listened, but I didn't even really notice until I thought about it later. Next it changed so it was mostly his mother's voice and then it got less serious and they were all laughing. It went back and forth like this for almost an hour, with things getting serious and then less serious. After a while we heard someone get up and we hurried as quietly as we could to the kitchen. Dad arrived in just as we had sat down at the kitchen table and said that we could come back to the living room.

Jackson's mum is some kind of genius, even better than Kira's mum because she actually sorts things out for you.

She had explained to my mum and dad about all the hours I had put in on the Blue Lavender Tea Palace and that I had learned to do ballroom dancing and was helping out some of the old people in the village. I found out in the car (Jackson's mum drove me to Aunt Maisie's) that Mum and Dad thought that I was just hanging around not doing anything and getting under Aunt Maisie's feet. She said my parents were very proud of what I'd been doing and that they all went on to have a chat about my school and how maybe it wasn't the best place for me.

'So I told your parents about how boarding school works so well for my two, because there are activities on all the time and Jackson's dad and I don't have to worry about being home late in the evenings.'

'So what did they say about that?' I asked. My head was spinning, because I never thought that they might agree to let me go away to school. That would be a dream come true, like this summer carried on all year.

'They said they would never send you to a mixed school as they wouldn't want you getting distracted ...'

(God, I can just hear them saying that, making me out to be a boy-crazed fiend!) '... but that an all-girls boarding school sounds like a good idea. They've asked me to look into some schools for them.'

'Jenny goes to a great boarding school,' I was so excited I started to prattle on for the next fifteen minutes all about it.

Too tired now to finish this. Very happy.

DAY 35

PARTY DAY!

I have to write this now, because you never know!

1, 2, 3, 4, 5, 6, 7, 8, 9, 10, 11, 12, 13, 14, 15,16, 17, 18, 19, 20, 21, 22, 23, 24, 25, 26, 27, 28, 29, 30, 31, 32, 33, 34, 35, 36, 37, 38, 39, 40, 41, 42, 43, 44, 45, 46, 47, 48, 49, 50, 51, 52, 53, 55, 56, 57, 58, 59, 60, 61, 62, 63, 64, 65, 66, 67, 68, 69, 70, 71, 72, 73, 74, 75, 76, 77, 78, 79, 80, 81, 82, 83, 84, 85, 86, 87, 88, 89, 90, 91, 92, 93, 94, 95, 96, 97, 98, 99, 100, 101, 102, 103, 104, 105, 106, 107, 108, 109, 110, 111, 112, 113, 114, 115, 116, 117, 118, 119, 120, 121, 122, 123, 124, 125, 126, 127, 128, 129, 130, 131, 132, 133, 134, 135, 136, 137, 138, 139, 140, 141, 142, 143, 144, 145, 146, 147, 148, 149, 150, 151, 152, 153, 154, 155, 156, 157, 158, 159, 160, 161,

162, 163, 164, 165, 166, 167, 168, 169, 170, 171,

172, 173, 174, 175, 176, 177, 178, 179, 180, 181,

181, 183, 184, 185, 186, 187, 188, 189, 190, 191,

192, 193, 194, 195, 196, 197, 198, 199, 200, 201,

202, 203, 204, 205, 206, 207, 208, 209, 210, 211,

212, 213, 214, 215, 216, 217, 218, 219, 220, 221,

222, 223, 224, 225, 226, 227, 228, 229, 230, 231,

232, 233, 234, 235, 236, 237, 238, 239, 240, 241,

242, 243, 244, 245, 246, 247, 248, 249, 250, 251,

252, 253, 254, 255, 256, 257, 258, 259, 260, 261,

262, 263, 264, 265, 266, 267, 268, 269, 270, 271,

272, 273, 274, 275, 276, 277, 278, 279, 280, 281,

282, 283, 284, 285, 286, 287, 288, 289, 290, 291,

292, 293, 294, 295, 296, 297, 298, 299, 300, 301,

302, 303, 304, 305, 306, 307, 308, 309, 310, 311,

312, 313, 314, 315, 316, 317, 318, 319, 320, 321,

322, 323, 324, 325, 326, 327, 328, 329, 330, 331,

332, 333, 334, 335, 336, 337, 338, 339, 340, 341,

342, 343, 344, 345, 346, 347, 348, 349, 350, 351,

352, 353, 354, 355, 356, 357, 358, 359, 360, 361,

362, 363, 364, 365, 366, 367, 368, 369, 370, 371,

372, 373, 374, 375, 376, 377, 378, 379, 380, 381,

382, 383, 384, 385, 386, 387, 388, 389, 390, 391,

392, 393, 394, 395, 396, 397, 398, 399, 400, 401,

402, 403, 404, 405, 406, 407, 408, 409, 410, 411,

412, 414, 415, 416, 417, 418, 419, 420, 421, 422,
423, 424, 425, 426, 427, 428, 429, 430, 431, 432,
433, 434, 435, 436, 437, 438, 439, 440, 441, 442,
443, 444, 445, 446, 447, 448, 449, 450, 451, 452,
453, 454, 455, 456, 457, 458, 459, 460, 461, 462,
463, 464, 465, 466, 467, 468, 469, 470, 471, 472,
473, 474, 475, 476, 477, 478, 479, 480, 481, 482,
483, 484, 485, 486, 487, 488, 489, 490, 491, 492,
493, 494, 495, 496, 497, 498, 499, 500!!!!!

488, 489, 490, 491, 492, 493, 494, 495, 496, 497, 498, 499, 500!!!!!

INTENSE DAYS 6

I don't know where to start, I want to write everything at once. Last night was so intense that I'm hoping that if I write it down it will feel more real. If anyone told me such things had happened to them, I'd go 'Yeah, right,' and think they were like the crazy lady who hangs out at the bus stop near our house talking about her dinner with the Queen of France.

Jenny and I got ready in my room. I didn't say anything to her about Jackson in case she thought Jackson just wanted to be my friend (rather than my 'more than just friend') and that would fairly slam the door on the dream. She is so optimistic that even if she said, 'I don't know', translated from Jenny-speak that would mean that she figured he had twenty other girls on a rota for the night. Also, she is *way* too excitable to hide things. Long story short, no talk of Jackson, lots of talk about Bob.

Jenny said she wasn't going to think about Bob 'in that way' so she wouldn't be disappointed if he went off with some other girl. I said if he did that, I would get the whole party to be quiet before introducing ... (drum roll) ... 'Bob and his famous, and now rarely performed, Armpit Fart Medley.' I couldn't believe he hadn't kissed her yet.

I decided that I'd make the whole Jackson thing a long-term plan and that if he didn't dance with me or kiss me this time around, I'd spend the whole year doing fascinating things, and having other boyfriends, and then next summer when I'd tell him what I'd been up to he'd realise how amazing I am and fall for me. Pathetic, I know! But what's a girl to do with more dress than hope?

So anyway, we looked incredible and we knew it. Aunt Maisie gave us a lift to the Park, after all, we couldn't just arrive down on our bikes. There were so many cars and catering vans and things that we walked from the gate after first dropping in quickly to show Nanny Gloria how we looked. She had been invited, but she said she preferred her gin rummy with her friends. I hoped she wouldn't drink too much.

There were about two hundred guests already, and more arriving by the minute. It was so surreal to see loads of people there when it's always just the four of us, like having tourists walk through your bedroom.

Mr Walsh was checking everyone's names at the gate. It was a bit ridiculous of him, the way he looked for our names even though he knew we were invited. I think he was pissed off that we were guests and he was working.

The main roadway to the Big House was edged with candles in lanterns and looked as if it was hundreds of years ago (except there were no horses around, just cars large enough to live in). The courtyard itself was like Christmas, with pink and blue lighting and the most luxurious table settings I have ever seen on dozens of long white-clothed tables, and silver-backed chairs. A small orchestra was playing on one half of the steps and I told Jenny she'd have to get used to having them play through every meal once she and Bob were married and living here! It was as if the weather had been designed too, warm with a very gentle breeze and probably the right number of millibars, whatever they're all about.

The buffet table was the whole length of the back of the courtyard, and full of all kinds of food, with a waiter behind each dish to explain it (in as non-condescending a way as possible) and serve you.

People were already eating, but I was too nervous to know what to do, I'm all forks in a setting like that. Jenny is used to fancy parties, so she grabbed a plate for her and one for me and soon mine was piled high (but not so high that I looked like I'd never eaten anything but porridge). I had duck, goose, dauphinoise potatoes, asparagus spears and some amazing vegetable mixture that I can't remember the name of. We were about to sit next to a lady in a long gold dress, but Bob called us over to where he was sitting with a load of people our age. I was so relieved, they were really friendly and fun and were eating, taking pictures, and talking and laughing with their mouths full, and I felt totally relaxed. I think it was Camille, Jeannie, Charles and Max I met then, but I got to know everyone as the meal went on.

Everyone was talking about real things, adventures they had been on, things they were learning and doing ... so different from me and my friends in town when we would just talk about whoever wasn't there. It was so exciting chatting with them and being a real part of it, that it was over two hours later that I noticed that Jackson was missing. I didn't want to be all obvious by asking anyone so I just suffered in silence, (and luxury!), and it wasn't even suffering, just intense wondering.

Then, I was sitting on a chair near the steps talking to Libby, who was the girl Jackson wanted me to get to know. She and Jenny already knew each other from school, but they didn't know that they both knew Jackson. We totally get each other's sense of humour, I guess that was why Jackson knew we'd like each other, and she's excited that I might be going to her school, (fingers massively crossed!)

As I sat there thinking about what a great and expensive time I was having, I felt someone touch my arm from behind. I can't even describe how I almost passed out as soon as I saw Jackson. He was dressed in full black tie like the other men (apparently 'full black tie' doesn't just mean the bow-tie, it means the whole black suit, and white shirt, and shiny shoes too), and his blond hair was still wild looking. He seemed to take a deep breath in when he saw me too, and I wouldn't make up something like that.

Anyway, Jackson wanted me to come away from the courtyard and there were no arguments from me!

He was using that military commander voice that he puts on when organising, and was steering me toward the lavender field. He said there were two men near the Blue Lavender Tea Palace keeping everyone away, telling them they couldn't come by until after the buffet. Even when Jackson explained who he was, they said it was their job to keep everyone away. That seemed normal to me if they wanted to keep people away from the Tea Palace until later, but Jackson said that there was something about the way they seemed panicked and wouldn't let him through although he was one of the people throwing the party that made him wonder.

'I saw one of them glance over to that big statue with the dolphins to the side of the Tea Palace, and whisper something into his walkie-talkie.'

'He was probably asking one of the waiters to save him some duck for later.'

'Tia, I need you to be serious.'

'Of course, I have my serious ball gown on.'

'Seriously serious. Focus!'

'OK.'

'That is a great dress, by the way.'

'Focus!'

So then, Jackson said that he'd suddenly remembered a story his mother had told him when he was little, about the base of that statue being the start of a passageway that ran underneath the Park, and how it was used in the olden days so the people in the Big House could escape the soldiers or king's men or whatever. Except Jackson told it better than that.

'And that time Buddy disappeared! Do you think...?'

'Exactly!' he said. 'I can't believe it didn't occur to me before now.'

I suppose an underground passageway is so overly obvious that you'd *never* think of it!

'Where would it lead to?' I asked, 'The gate?'

As soon as I said that, he grabbed my arm and started walking fast in the opposite direction. For a second I thought I had said something wrong and he was bringing me back to the buffet, but then I realised we were heading for the stone hut.

'I bet those weren't rats we heard,' he said as we reached the hut, and he got down on his hands and knees, not caring for one second about his lovely suit. He pulled at one of the floorboards until it gave way and came out completely.

I said, 'Let's go down.'

'I knew you'd say that,' he grinned.

We disappeared down the hole, helped by this rope ladder hanging there. I went first, not because I was feeling brave, but because I didn't want Jackson to be able to look up my dress, but I didn't tell him that.

It was really strange, like being in an adventure book, but it was real life. I was shaking. The corridor at the bottom was lit by these little flashlight things and was painted white to make it all brighter. Now we knew what the extra paint was all about. After a while we got to this big white room filled with boxes and boxes of electrical goods and clothes.

We could hear men's voices coming from the other end of the corridor so we legged it back the way we came (Jackson going first up the ladder) and back to the Big House, where the dinner seemed to be ending.

As the rest of the party-goers started to make their way over to the Blue Lavender Tea Palace to dance, Jackson headed round the back to the Big House to fetch his bike. We decided not to phone because we couldn't be sure who was in on it, and who was listening. And that's how I ended up with my long dress hitched up into my hand on the crossbar of a bike with a guy in a dress suit, all the way to the village police station. The police were great. They laughed at us at first and then they started to really listen. They made us go through everything carefully and then called to the nearest town for backup.

They told us that this part of the country has been well known for the past couple of years as a place where smugglers hide their stuff for months at a time before moving it on to sell.

I thought it was a daft idea, smugglers in this day and age and us nowhere near the sea. They explained that if people bring goods in legally they have to pay high taxes and duty, but if they avoid paying the money to the customs people they have more to keep for themselves.

Anyway, an hour later we arrived back at the party in a police car and there was a police van already waiting. It was so like a TV show or something, with all the guests talking away, wondering what was going on as the two tunnel-guarding men were led away, followed five minutes later by some men who had been in the tunnel, including Mr Walsh. Bob and Jenny were standing beside us by then and we told them what was going on. It was *so* fast, like a circus or something. Jenny went off to reassure the guests while Bob went to explain to his parents and relatives. Luckily the grandfather had gone to bed directly after the dinner.

As they led Mr Walsh away I noticed a streak of oil on the back of his trousers, just like the one I had got on my new skirt.

'The warehouse!' I said, and Jackson explained to the police that they might like to check the old oil-storage warehouse in the village.

We found out a while later that the other man was there, the one I had seen arguing with Mr Walsh, and I had to formally identify him, so the four of us were up all night, giving statements and explaining to worried adults and everything.

It is now noon and I haven't slept and I am back in Aunt Maisie's house. It was amazing, but I'm a bit pissed off that the counting to five hundred thing doesn't work.

DAY 37

I stayed awake until three yesterday afternoon and then slept until six a.m. this morning. I got dressed slowly (jeans, runners and the new pink top) and then rode over with Buddy to see Jenny. Bob had kissed her while they were on the dance floor, right before the police got there, and again when he walked her home. I'm so happy for her and made her tell it about a million times. It was just what I had dreamed for me and Jackson, them waltzing and talking about the work we had done on the place, and then Bob said she deserved to be kissed for all her efforts with a paintbrush.

I found out that gin rummy is a card game for old ladies and not a drink. Nanny Gloria taught myself and Jenny how to play to distract us when we got all jumpy and wanted to hang out in the Tea Palace. She said it wouldn't be 'dignified' to go up there so soon after the party, and I guess she was right because what we were hoping for is not that dignified if done right!

Bob and Jackson phoned us around lunchtime to tell us that they were being kept busy organising, and getting the Big House and the Tea Palace back in order. The police told them that Mr Walsh and the men had used the cover of all the catering trucks to add a couple of trucks of their own (filled with the smuggled stuff), and knew that the noise and bustle of a party would hide what they were doing, especially as there were so many young people running around the Park at night, (which took some explaining to Bob's dad.) The man at the warehouse was the head of a gang that stretched right across the whole continent so they were thrilled to finally be able to link him to the goods.

Tired again.

DAY 38

Today I was feeling a bit disappointed that all the excitement was over. Then I opened the door and there on the doorstep was a big bunch of lavender, like before! This time the note was unsigned and said to come to the Blue Lavender Tea Palace at nine o'clock tonight and to wear my special dress. I changed at Jenny's and made sure I looked as good as the other night.

When I got to the Tea Palace I saw that although most of the decorations and things had been removed, the party lights were still up, and the whole thing looked magical. Jackson was standing there in his suit and we couldn't stop smiling at each other. He had music playing from a music system, and didn't say a word to me, just took my hand and waltzed with me around the dance floor, and then we did a foxtrot and another waltz, (thank God not a rumba, because I look like a stunned chicken doing that). He held me really close, like he didn't care about having the hold right; I didn't care either, I just wanted to be near him. He said he had wanted to dance with me ever since I called him those very-bad-but-creative names the first time we met, since the first time he saw my eyes full of fire. I told him I had wanted to dance with him since, 'Ohhh, about Wednesday,' and he laughed and said that no-one has a brain quite like mine and that I wasn't getting away this time.

Then we went for a walk in the lavender field and he just pulled me close and kissed me. It's the first time I've been kissed without a million other people around and rock music blaring and it was VERY nice. In fact they need to invent a whole new word for how nice it was.

He loved it when he noticed that I was wearing my old black boots underneath the dress, and I explained that those other kinds of shoes are great, but not for having adventures in. For some reason that made him kiss me again.

We were talking laughing and kissing and dancing until it was almost midnight and I had to do my Cinderella act again. I can't *believe* it. I'm going to just lie here and think about it for hours.

THE LAST DAY OF THIS JOURNAL, FIRST NEW DAY OF MY FABULOUS LIFE

In the last two weeks since the party there have been so many family meetings and phone calls and goodbyes. I don't feel the same need to write in this diary now as I feel so excited and happy, instead of angry and annoyed like before. The *great* news is that I am going to the same boarding school as Jenny, starting next week! They do such *amazing* subjects, I even get to learn to play the electric guitar! I get to do ballet too, which will help with my ballroom dancing. Jenny and Libby and I have applied to room together and have made a pact to work hard and be top of the year, which will definitely be a first for me! They say it's a cool place, that you actually want to do the stuff because they make it so interesting.

I just got my school book list and there's a hundred things on there, but I know I can do it. Especially as the first novel I need to read for English is *Jane Eyre*!! Sorted!

The old couple have moved into a seniors' centre and can't take Buddy, so I get to *keep* him! They told me they'd miss him, but they knew I'd look after him really well. I think he's one of the things I'm happiest about! He may be a funny-looking dog, but he's *MY* dog now, and I love him. My new school has a kennel for dogs so I don't have to worry about Mum developing any mysterious allergies!

I have been at home for the last week, and I now bring my mum a cup of tea every morning and she loves that, and we chat for a few minutes before she starts her day. I have been helping out a bit at the kids' club she runs for the church and I really get why she stays late, there's so much to get done. She loves the meals I've been cooking too, and Aidan is home so he's been teaching me even *more* recipes.

When I told Dad about how I learned to ballroom dance, he pulled back the sofa and did a quickstep with me. I had *no* idea he could do that! Then he showed me the train tickets they have bought to get me home from school every second weekend. I think that I'll get on much better with them this way, I won't get so grumpy and take them for granted. Dad and I are even having conversations, mostly about ordinary things, but I like that.

I know I'll miss Kira and Dee, but you do need to move on with your own life sometimes. I like them a lot, I just don't really like myself when I'm with them.

I am allowed to go to Aunt Maisie's for mid-term, and Jackson is working on his parents so he can be at the Big House at the same time. Jenny will be with her parents in New York for that week, but she says that Jackson and Bob's school and ours are always meeting up for dances and debates and sports matches, so we'll all be back together really soon.

I am sitting in the same room as when the power cut happened. It's the same room, but so much better. It's funny how the whole world changed when I did.

**Hope you enjoyed Tia's story,
now meet Tammy in *Copper Girl***

MAY
30

I wish I was international, you know, jet set and everything. That way I could be booking a plane ticket somewhere and not just sitting in the bedroom I've had for the past fourteen years re-reading my text messages. 'Chat 2 ya! Mmwah! CU xxx'; that's all it said, like she was going off to dance class and I'd see her after!

I was minding the shop when it first came through and I was so angry I almost threw the phone at the Pringles display. I thought that it should *mean* something to her that our little group is being split up, at least for the summer. Charlie's Dad is *such* a pain; he hasn't even called her much since Christmas, but then he sends for her to join him in Canada without even thinking that she might have a life. What pisses me off most is that Charlie didn't seem to care about months of being ignored by him and all those conversations we had about it, instead she got all excited about Vancouver and sailing and her Dad's dog and stuff and didn't even ask me how I was going to survive on my own.

I spent this evening downstairs minding the shop, pretending to study and dying to get back to my room so I could cry. My eyes kept welling up and I had to pretend to all the regulars that I had hayfever.

At least Hellie will be around for another week, but then it's worse because she doesn't expect to be back *EVER*. She's another one who could work a bit harder at being upset! You'd swear all this was normal. And it's worst for me because I'll be doing the same things as usual except on my own. They'll be having real adventures and meeting amazing people.

They are the best friends I've ever had and at fifteen I'm way too old for getting new ones. I can't think of one other person I know who I could stand for more than a minute-and-a-half.

I don't want Mum to hear me crying in case she thinks it's about Gran and gets all upset herself. I mean, I *am* still upset about that, but I find I can only really cry about one thing at a time, otherwise I get all confused, and the tears stop, and I just feel a more muddy kind of awful.

I have started writing this because last night I saw a film about a girl who found a diary that a girl wrote two hundred years ago and it was *really* interesting. Maybe this will be interesting in the twenty-third century, because God knows there is nothing good about my life right now. In fact the best thing is Johnny Saunders and I only ever walk past him at the bus stop and don't even say anything. Next week I won't even have that, because the exams will be over.

Maybe I should explain about cars and microwaves and iPods and all that, but I suppose they will have better history books in two centuries time, so they won't need those kinds of details from me. I would *love* it if I was important or did something like a really historical person.

Copper Girl by Judy May, Out Now!

Copper Girl by Judy May, 2006

ISBN-10: 0-86278-990-7

ISBN:-13: 978-0-86278-990-9

For other great O'Brien books check out our website